PRAISE FOR THE FALLEN SERIES
BY LAUREN KATE

'A romantic but dark tale for teenagers' *Express*

'Dark and romantic, an absolute blinder of a book' *Sun*

'A beautifully gripping love story' *Bliss*

'Sexy, fascinating and scary'
P. C. Cast, author of the *House of Night* series

'No one writes love like Kate does' *Once Upon a Bookcase*

'One of the most hotly anticipated books
of the year' *The Bookseller*

'Guaranteed to thrill and delight in
equal measure' *Love Reading*

'Adrenaline fuelled . . . Five stars' *The Bookbag*

AND FROM HER FANS . . .

'a piece of genius' *Hayley*

'these books are going to bury vampires
six feet under' *Abbigale*

'this book is just as good as *Twilight*,
if not better' *Taunya*

'An amazingly be
privileged jus

D1350124

www.fallenbooks.co.uk

Also by Lauren Kate:

FALLEN
TORMENT
PASSION
RAPTURE
FALLEN IN LOVE

THE BETRAYAL OF
NATALIE HARGROVE

FALLEN

IN

LOVE

NEW TALES FROM THE
FALLEN WORLD

LAUREN KATE

CORGI

FALLEN IN LOVE
A CORGI BOOK 978 0 552 56609 4

First published in Great Britain by Doubleday,
an imprint of Random House Children's Publishers UK
A Random House Group Company

Doubleday edition published 2012
Corgi edition published 2012

3 5 7 9 10 8 6 4

Copyright © Tinderbox Books, LLC and Lauren Kate, 2012

The right of Lauren Kate to be identified as the author of this work has been asserted in
accordance with the Copyright, Designs and Patents Act 1988.

All rights reserved. No part of this publication may be reproduced,
stored in a retrieval system, or transmitted in any form or by any means, electronic,
mechanical, photocopying, recording or otherwise,
without the prior permission of the publishers.

The Random House Group Limited supports the Forest Stewardship Council®
(FSC®), the leading international forest-certification organisation. Our books
carrying the FSC label are printed on FSC®-certified paper. FSC is the only
forest-certification scheme supported by the leading environmental organisations,
including Greenpeace. Our paper procurement policy can be found at
www.randomhouse.co.uk/environment

Set in Palatino

Corgi Books are published by Random House Children's Publishers UK,
61–63 Uxbridge Road, London W5 5SA

www.randomhousechildrens.co.uk
www.totallyrandombooks.co.uk
www.randomhouse.co.uk

Addresses for companies within The Random House Group Limited
can be found at: www.randomhouse.co.uk/offices.htm

THE RANDOM HOUSE GROUP Limited Reg. No. 954009

A CIP catalogue record for this book is available
from the British Library.

Printed and bound by CPI Group (UK) Ltd, Croydon, CR0 4YY

FOR MY READERS,

WHO HAVE SHOWN ME SO MANY KINDS OF LOVE

FALLEN

IN

LOVE

The life so brief, the art so long in the learning, the attempt so hard, the conquest so sharp, the fearful joy that ever slips away so quickly—by all this I mean love, which so sorely astounds my feeling with its wondrous operation, that when I think upon it I scarce know whether I wake or sleep.

⹉⹊

—GEOFFREY CHAUCER, *The Parliament of Fowls*
Translated by Gerard NeCastro

LOVE WHERE YOU LEAST EXPECT IT

THE VALENTINE OF
SHELBY AND MILES

ONE

TWO FOR THE ROAD

Shelby and Miles were laughing when they stepped out of the Announcer. Its dark tendrils clung to the brim of Miles's blue Dodgers baseball cap and Shelby's tangled ponytail as the two of them emerged.

Even though Shelby's body felt as weary as if she'd done four back-to-back sessions of Vinyasa yoga, at least she and Miles were back on solid—present-tense—ground. Home. *Finally.*

The air was cold, the sky gray but bright. Miles's

shoulders towered in front of her, shielding her body from the brisk wind that sent ripples across the white T-shirt he'd been wearing since they'd left Luce's parents' backyard on Thanksgiving.

Eons ago.

"I'm serious!" Shelby was saying. "Why is it so hard for you to believe that my first priority is lip balm?" She ran a finger across her lip and recoiled exaggeratedly. "They're like sandpaper!"

"You're crazy." Miles snorted, but his eyes followed Shelby's finger as she gingerly traced her lower lip. "*Lip balm* is what you missed inside the Announcers?"

"And my podcasts," Shelby said, crunching over a pile of dead gray leaves. "And my sun salutations on the beach—"

They had been leapfrogging through the Announcers for so long: from the cell in the Bastille where they'd met a wraithlike prisoner who wouldn't give his name; into and right back out of a bloody Chinese battlefield where they didn't recognize a soul; and, most recently, from Jerusalem, where they'd found Daniel at last, looking for Luce. Only Daniel wasn't entirely himself. He was joined—literally—with some ghostly past version of himself. And he hadn't been able to set himself free.

Shelby couldn't stop thinking about Miles and Daniel fencing with the starshots, about the way Daniel's two bodies—past and present—had been wrenched apart after Miles drew the arrow down the angel's chest.

Creepy things happened inside Announcers; Shelby was glad to be done with them. Now if they could just not get lost in these woods on their way back to their dorm. Shelby looked toward what she hoped was west and started to lead Miles through the dreary unfamiliar section of the forest. "Shoreline should be this way."

The return home was bittersweet.

She and Miles had entered the Announcer with a mission; they'd jumped through in Luce's parents' backyard after Luce herself had disappeared. They'd gone after her to bring her home—as Miles said, Announcers weren't to be pranced into lightly—but also just to make sure she was all right. Whatever Luce was to the angels and demons fighting over her, Shelby and Miles didn't care. To them, she was a friend.

But on their hunt, they kept just missing her. It had driven Shelby nuts. They'd gone from one bizarre stop to the next and still had seen no sign of Luce.

She and Miles had bickered several times over which way to go and how to get there—and Shelby hated fighting with Miles. It was like arguing with a puppy. The truth was, neither of them really knew what they were doing.

But in Jerusalem, there had been one good thing: The three of them—Shelby, Miles, and Daniel—had actually, for once, gotten along. Now, with Daniel's blessing (some might call it a command), Shelby and Miles were finally headed back home. Part of Shelby worried about abandoning Luce, but another part—the part that trusted Daniel—was eager to get back to where she was supposed to be. Her proper era and place.

It felt like they had been traveling for a very long time, but who knew how time worked inside the Announcers? Would they come back and find they'd been gone just seconds, Shelby had wondered, a bit nervously, or would *years* have passed?

"As soon as we get back to Shoreline," Miles said, "I'm running straight into a long, hot shower."

"Yeah, good call." Shelby grabbed a chunk of her thick blond ponytail and sniffed. "Wash this Announcer funk out of my hair. If that's even possible."

"You know what?" Miles leaned in, lowering his voice, even though there was no one else around. Weird that the Announcer had planted them so far off the grounds of the school. "Maybe tonight we should sneak into the mess hall and snag some of those flaky biscuits—"

"The buttery ones? From the tube?" Shelby's eyes widened. Another genius idea from Miles. The guy was good to have around. "Man, I've missed Shoreline. It's good to be—"

They crossed beyond the line of trees. A meadow opened up before them. And then it hit Shelby: She wasn't seeing any of the familiar Shoreline buildings, because they weren't there.

She and Miles were . . . somewhere else.

She paused and glanced at the hillside surrounding them. Snow sat on the boughs of trees that Shelby suddenly realized were definitely *not* California redwoods. And the slushy mud road ahead of them was no Pacific Coast Highway. It wound downward over the hillside for several miles toward a stunningly old-looking city protected by a massive black stone wall.

It reminded her of one of those faded old tapestries where unicorns frolicked in front of medieval towns, which some ex-boyfriend of her mom had once dragged her to see at the Getty.

"I thought we were home!" Shelby cried, her voice landing somewhere between a bark and a whine. Where *were* they?

She stopped just short of the crude road and looked around at the muddy desolation before her. There was *no one* around. Scary.

"I thought we were, too." Miles scratched his cap glumly. "I guess we're not quite back at Shoreline."

"*Not quite?* Look at this excuse for a road. Look at that fortress thing down there." She gasped. "And are those little moving dots *knights*? Unless we're in some kind of theme park, we're stuck in the freaking Middle Ages!" She covered her mouth. "We'd better not get the plague. Whose Announcer did you open up in Jerusalem, anyway?"

"I don't know, I just—"

"We're never going to get home!"

"Yes, we are, Shel. I read about this . . . I think. We got backwards in time by leapfrogging through other angels' Announcers, so maybe we have to get home that way, too."

"Well, what are you waiting for? Open another one!"

"It's not like that." Miles jerked his baseball cap lower over his eyes. Shelby could barely see his face. "I think we have to find one of the angels, and just sort of borrow another shadow—"

"You make it sound like borrowing a sleeping bag for a camping trip."

"Listen: If we find a shadow that casts across the century where we actually exist, we can make it home."

"How do we do *that*?"

Miles shook his head. "I thought I'd done it when we were with Daniel in Jerusalem."

"I'm scared." Shelby crossed her arms over her chest and shivered in the wind. "Just do *something*!"

"I can't just—especially not with you screaming at me—"

"Miles!" Shelby's body seized up. What was that rumbling sound behind them? Something was coming up the road.

"*What?*"

A horse-drawn cart creaked toward them. The clop of horses' hooves was growing louder. In a second, whoever was driving that cart would crest the hill and see them.

"Hide!" Shelby screamed.

The silhouette of a stout man holding the reins of two brown-and-white-spotted horses rose into view on the sloping road. Shelby grabbed Miles by his collar. He'd been fussing nervously with his hat, and as she yanked him behind the wide trunk of an oak tree, the bright blue cap flew off his head.

Shelby watched the cap—the cap that had been part of Miles's daily wardrobe for years—sail through the air like a blue jay. Then it plummeted downward, into a wide pale-brown puddle of mud in the road.

"My hat," Miles whispered.

They were huddled very close together, their backs against the rough bark of the oak. Shelby glanced over at him and was amazed to see his face in its entirety. His eyes seemed magnified. His hair messy. He looked . . . handsome, like a guy she'd never met before. Miles tugged on his hat-hair, self-conscious.

Shelby cleared her throat and her thoughts. "We'll get it as soon as the cart goes by. Just stay out of sight until this dude is out of the way."

She could feel Miles's warm breath on her neck and the jut of his hipbone pushing against her side. How was

Miles so skinny? The guy ate like a horse, but he was all meat and no potatoes. At least, that was what Shelby's mother would say if she ever met him—which she never would if Miles couldn't find an Announcer that would take them back to the present.

Miles fidgeted, straining to see his cap.

"Stay still," Shelby said. "This guy could be some sort of barbarian."

Miles held up a finger and tilted his head. "Listen. He's *singing*."

A patch of snow crunched under Shelby's feet as she craned her neck around the tree to watch the cart approach. The driver was a ruddy-cheeked man with a dirty shirt collar, daggy trousers that were obviously handmade, and a colossal fur vest he wore cinched at the waist with a leather belt. His small blue felt cap looked like a ridiculous little polka dot in the center of his broad, bald forehead.

His song had the jolly, raucous ring of a pub tune—and boy, was he belting it out. The clopping of his horses' hooves sounded almost like a drumming accompaniment to his loud, brassy voice:

"Riding to town t' fetch a maid, a busty maid, a lusty maid. Riding to town to take a bride, in eventide, a Valentine!"

"Classy." Shelby rolled her eyes. But at least she recognized the man's accent, a clue. "So, I guess we're in jolly old England."

"And I guess it's Valentine's Day," Miles said.

"Thrilling. Twenty-four hours of feeling especially single and pathetic . . . *medieval-style*."

She'd done jazz hands on that last bit for effect, but Miles was too busy watching the crude board cart drive by to notice.

The horses were tacked in unmatched blue and white bridles and harnesses. Their ribs were showing. The man rode alone, sitting atop a rotting wooden bench at the head of the cart, which was about the size of a truck bed and covered with a sturdy white tarp. Shelby couldn't see what the man was hauling to town, but whatever it was, it was heavy. The horses were sweating despite the frigid weather, and the planks of wood at the cart's base strained and shuddered as it drove toward the walled city.

"We should follow him," Miles said.

"What for?" Shelby's mouth twitched. "Want to fetch yourself a busty, lusty maid?"

"I'd like to 'fetch' someone we know, whose Announcer we can use to get us home. Remember? Your lip balm?" He parted her lips with his thumb. His touch left Shelby momentarily speechless. "We'll have a better shot coming across one of the angels in town."

The cart's wheels groaned in and out of ruts in the muddy road, rocking the driver from side to side. Soon he was close enough that Shelby could see the coarseness of his beard, which was as thick and black as his bearskin vest. His pitch faltered on the extended last syllable of *Valentine,* and he took a great gulp of air before beginning again. Then his song broke off abruptly.

"What's this?" he grunted.

Shelby could see that his hands were chapped and red from the cold as they tugged roughly on the horses' reins to slow them. The rail-thin animals neighed, coming to a stop just short of Miles's bright blue baseball cap.

"No, no, no," Shelby muttered under her breath. Miles's face had gone pale.

The man shimmied fatly off the bench, his boots landing in the thick mud. He walked toward Miles's hat, bent down with another grunt, and swooped it up in the blink of an eye.

Shelby heard Miles swallow hard.

A quick swipe against the man's already filthy trousers and the cap was halfway clean. Without a word, he turned and mounted the cart's bench again, tucking the hat inside the tarp behind him.

Shelby looked down at herself and her green hoodie. She tried to imagine this man's reaction if she were to pop out from behind a tree wearing weird clothes from the future and try to take back his prize. It was not a calming idea.

In the time it had taken Shelby to chicken out, the man had tugged on the reins; the cart started rolling to town again, and his song entered its twelfth off-key round.

Another thing Shelby had screwed up. "Oh, Miles. I'm sorry."

"Now we definitely have to follow him," Miles said, a little desperate.

"Really?" Shelby asked. "It's just a hat."

But then she looked at Miles. She still wasn't used to seeing his face. The cheeks Shelby used to think of as babyish seemed stronger, more angular, and his irises were speckled with a new intensity. She could tell by his crestfallen expression that it definitely wasn't "just a hat" to him. Whether it held special memories or was simply a good-luck talisman, she didn't know. But she would do anything to get that look off his face.

"Okay," she blurted out. "Let's go get it."

Before Shelby knew what was happening, Miles had slipped his hand through hers. It felt strong and assured and a little impulsive—and then he tugged her toward the road. "Come on!" She resisted for an instant, but then her eyes accidentally locked with Miles's, and they were super-crazy blue, and Shelby felt a wave of exhilaration kick in.

Then they were running down a snow-dotted medieval road, moving past crop fields that were dead for the winter, covered in a sleek sheet of white that draped the trees and spotted the dirt road. They were heading toward a walled city with towering black spires and a narrow, moated entry. Hand in hand, pink-cheeked, chapped-lipped, laughing for no reason Shelby could ever have put into words—laughing so hard she nearly forgot what they were about to do. But then, when Miles called out, "Jump!"—something snapped into place and she did.

For a moment, it almost felt like she was flying.

A knotty log formed the back ledge of the cart, barely wide enough to balance on. Their feet skimmed it, landing there by sheer, graceless luck—

For a moment. Then the cart hit a rut and rattled fiercely, and Miles's foot slipped and Shelby lost her grip on the canvas tarp. Her fingers slipped and her body flailed and she and Miles were flung backward, sailing downward, into the mud.

Splash.

Shelby grunted. Her rib cage throbbed. She wiped the cold mud from her eyes and spat out a mouthful of the dingy stuff. She looked up at the cart growing smaller in the distance. Miles's hat was gone.

"Are you okay?" she asked him.

He wiped his face with the hem of his T-shirt. "Yeah. You?" When she nodded, he grinned. "Do Francesca's face if she found out where we were right now." Miles's command sounded cheerful, but Shelby knew that inside he was gutted.

Still, she would play along. Shelby loved to impersonate their stately Shoreline teacher. She rolled out of the puddle, propped herself on her elbows, stuck out her chest, and pinched up her nose. "And I suppose you're going to deny that you were purposely attempting to disgrace Shoreline's legacy? I'm absolutely *loath* to imagine what the faaancypants board of directors will say. And have I mentioned that I broke a nail on an Announcer's edge trying to track you two down—"

"Now, now, Frankie." Miles helped Shelby up from the mud as he deepened his voice to do his best impersonation of Steven, Francesca's slightly more relaxed demon husband. "Let's not be too hard on the Nephilim. A single semester of scrubbing toilets really should teach them their lesson. After all, their mistake began with noble intentions."

Noble intentions. Finding Luce.

Shelby swallowed, feeling a somberness settle over her. They'd been a team, the three of them. Teams stuck together.

"We *didn't* give up on her," Miles said softly. "You heard what Daniel said. He is the only one who can find her."

"You think he's found her yet?"

"I hope so. He said he would. But—"

"But what?" Shelby asked.

Miles paused. "Luce was pretty mad when she left

everyone in the backyard. I hope that whenever Daniel finds her, she forgives him."

Shelby stared at mud-slicked Miles, knowing how much he had—at one point—truly cared about Luce. Admittedly, Shelby hadn't ever felt *that* way about anyone. In fact, she was legendary for choosing the absolute worst guys to date. *Phil?* Come on! If she hadn't fallen for him, the Outcasts wouldn't have tracked Luce down and she wouldn't have had to jump through the Announcer, and Miles and Shelby wouldn't be stuck here right now. Covered in mud.

But that wasn't the point. The point was: Shelby was amazed that Miles wasn't more bitter about seeing Luce in mega-love with someone else. But he wasn't. That was Miles.

"She'll forgive him," Shelby finally said. "If someone loved me enough to dive through multiple millennia just to find me, I'd get over myself."

"Oh, that's all it would take?" Miles elbowed her.

On impulse, she swatted his stomach with the back of her hand. It was the way she and her mom teased each other, like best friends or something. But Shelby was usually a lot more reserved with people outside her nuclear family. Weird.

"Hey." Miles interrupted her thoughts. "Right now you and I need to focus on getting to town, finding an angel who can help us, and making our way home."

And getting that hat in the meantime, Shelby added

inside her head as she and Miles broke into a jog, following the cart toward the city.

❄❄

The tavern stood about a mile outside the city walls, the lone establishment in a large field. It was a small wooden structure with a swinging sign of weathered wood, and big barrels of ale lined up against its walls.

Shelby and Miles had jogged past hundreds of trees stripped of their leaves by the cold, and melting patches of muddy snow on the pocked, winding road to the city. There really wasn't all that much to see. In fact, they had even lost sight of the cart after Shelby got a stitch in her side and had to slow down, but now, serendipitously, they spotted it parked outside the tavern.

"That's our guy," Shelby said under her breath. "He probably stopped in for a drink. Sucker. We'll just snatch the hat back and be on our way."

Miles nodded, but as they slipped around the back of the cart, Shelby spotted the man in the fur vest inside the doorway, and her heart sank. She couldn't hear what he was saying, but he held Miles's hat in his hands and was showing it off to the innkeeper as proudly as if it were a rare gem.

"Oh," Miles said, disappointed. Then he straightened his shoulders. "You know what, I'll get another one. You can buy them everywhere in California."

"Mmmm, right." Shelby swatted the canvas tarp of

❄ 17 ❄

the man's wagon in frustration. The force of her blow sent a corner billowing up. For just a second, she caught a glimpse of a heap of boxes inside.

"Hmm." She snaked her head under the tarp.

Underneath, it was cold and a little fetid, crammed with odds and ends. There were wooden cages filled with sleeping speckled hens, heavy sacks of feed, a burlap bag of mismatched iron tools, and loads of wooden boxes. She tried the lid of one of the boxes, but it wouldn't budge.

"What are you doing?" Miles asked.

Shelby gave a crooked smile. "Having an idea." Reaching for something that looked like a small crowbar in the sack of tools, she pried open the lid of the closest box. "That's a bingo."

"Shelby?"

"If we're going into town, these clothes might make the wrong statement." She flicked the pocket of her green hoodie for effect. "Don't you think?"

Back under the tarp she found some simple garments, which looked faded and worn, probably outgrown by the driver's family back home. She tossed little gems out at Miles, who scrambled to catch everything.

Soon, he held a long, pale-green linen gown with bell sleeves and an embroidered golden strip running down its center, a pair of lemon-yellow stockings, and a bonnet that looked sort of like a nun's wimple, made of taupe linen.

"But what are *you* going to wear?" Miles joked.

Shelby had to rummage through a half dozen more boxes full of rags, bent nails, and smooth stones before she found anything that would work for Miles. Finally, she pulled out a simple blue robe made of stiff, coarse wool. It would keep him warm against this buffeting wind; it was long enough to cover his Nikes; and for some reason it occurred to Shelby that the color was perfect for his eyes.

Shelby unzipped her green hoodie and slung it over the back of the cart. Goose bumps rose on her bare arms as she tugged the billowing dress over her jeans and tank top.

Miles still looked reluctant. "I feel weird stealing stuff that guy was probably taking into town to sell," he whispered.

"Karma, Miles. He stole your hat."

"No, he *found* my hat. What if he's got a family to support?"

Shelby whistled under her breath. "You'd never make it a day on Skid Row, kid"—she shrugged—"unless you had me there to look after you. Look, compromise, we'll repay something else to the cosmos. My sweater . . ." She chucked the green hoodie into the box. "Who knows? Maybe hoodies will be all the rage next season in the anatomy theaters, or whatever they do for fun around here."

Miles held the taupe bonnet above Shelby's head.

But it wouldn't fit over her ponytail, so he tugged on the elastic band. Her blond hair tumbled down her shoulders. Now *she* felt self-conscious. Her hair was a complete beast. She *never* wore it down. But Miles's eyes lit up as he placed the bonnet on her head.

"M'lady." He gallantly held out his hand. "Might I have the pleasure of accompanying you into this fair city?"

If Luce had been here, back when all three of them were still just good friends and things were a little less complicated, Shelby would have known just how to joke back. Luce would have put on her sweet, demure damsel-in-distress voice and called Miles her knight in shining armor or some crap like that, to which Shelby could have added something sarcastic, and then everyone would have burst out laughing, and the weird tension Shelby felt across her shoulders, the tightness in her chest—it would have gone away. Everything would have felt *normal*, whole.

But it was just Shelby and Miles.

Together. Alone.

They turned to face the black stone walls around the city, which surrounded a high central keep. Marigold-colored flags hung from iron poles in the tall stone tower. The air smelled like coal and moldy hay. Music came from inside the walls—a lyre maybe, some soft-skinned drums. And somewhere in there, Shelby hoped, was an angel whose Announcer could take the two of them back to the present, where they belonged.

Miles was still holding out his hand, gazing at her like he had no idea how deep blue his eyes were. She took a deep breath and slipped her palm inside his. He gave her hand a little squeeze and the two of them strolled into town.

TWO

BIZARRE BAZAAR

Gone was the peaceful countryside. Instead, just outside the city gates, there was a great bustling, with makeshift tents set up along the green—which was more a grayish brown now, in winter—on both sides of the road leading to the tall black city walls. The tents were clearly part of a temporary setup, like a weekend-long festival or something. The happy chaos of the people milling around reminded Shelby a little of Bonnaroo, which she had seen pictures of on the Internet. She studied what people were wearing—apparently the wimple look was in. She didn't think she and Miles stuck out *too* badly.

They joined the crowd passing through the gates and followed the flow of people, which seemed to move in only one direction: toward the market in the central square. Turrets rose before them, part of a grand castle near the far limits of the city walls. The square's cornerstone was a modest but attractive early-Gothic church (Shelby recognized the spindly towers). A maze of narrow gray streets and alleys sliced off from the market square, which was crowded, chaotic, stinking, and vibrant, the kind of place where you went to find anything and anyone.

"Linen! Two bolts for tenpence!"

"Candlesticks! One of a kind!"

"Barley beer! Fresh barley beer!"

Shelby and Miles had to leap out of the way to avoid the stocky friar pushing a cart with earthenware jugs of barley beer. They watched his broad, gray-robed back as he cut a path through the crowded market. Shelby started to follow him, just to get a little space, but a moment later, the smelly mass of chattering citizens filled the gap.

It was nearly impossible to take a step without bumping into someone.

There were so many people in the square—haggling,

gossiping, swatting children's thieving hands away from the apples for sale—that no one paid attention to Miles and Shelby at all.

"How are we ever going to find anyone we know in this cesspool?" Shelby held tight to Miles's hand as the tenth person stepped on her foot. This was worse than that Green Day concert in Oakland where Shelby bruised two ribs in the mosh pit.

Miles craned his neck. "I don't know. Maybe everyone knows everyone else?" He was taller than most of the citizens, so it wasn't as bad for him.

He had fresh air and a clear sight line, but *she* was feeling a claustrophobic fit coming on: She felt the telltale flush creep across her cheeks. Frantically, she tugged at the high collar of her dress, hearing a few stitches snap. "How do people breathe in these things?"

"In through your nose, out through your mouth," Miles instructed, demonstrating his own advice for a second before the stench forced him to wrinkle his nose. "Er. Look, there's a well over there. How about a drink?"

"We'll probably get cholera," Shelby muttered, but he was already moving away, pulling her behind him.

They dipped under a sagging clothesline damp with homespun clothes, stepped over a small parade of scraggly, clucking black roosters, and angled past a pair of redheaded brothers peddling pears before they ended up at the well. It was an archaic thing—a ring of stones around a hole, with a wooden tripod set up over the opening. A mossy bucket dangled from a primitive pulley.

After a few seconds, Shelby could breathe again. "People drink from that thing?"

Now she could see that though the market took up most of the open square, it wasn't the only show in town. A group of medieval mannequins robed in burlap had been set up on one side of the well. Young boys practiced wielding wooden swords, tilting at the ancestors of crash-test dummies like knights in training. Wandering minstrels strolled the edges of the market, singing strangely pretty songs. Even the well was its own little destination.

She saw now that there was a wooden crank to raise the bucket. A boy in skintight buckskin leggings had dipped a ladle of water from the bucket and was holding it out to a girl with enormous wide-set eyes and a holly branch tucked behind her ear. She drained the ladle in a few thirsty gulps, gazing lovingly at the boy the whole time, oblivious to the water dripping down her chin and onto her beautiful cream gown.

When she was finished, the boy passed the ladle to Miles with a wink. Shelby wasn't sure she liked what that wink insinuated, but she was too thirsty to make a scene.

"Here for the St. Valentine's Faire, are you?" the girl asked Shelby in a voice as placid as a lake.

"I, uh, we—"

"Indeed," Miles jumped in, adopting a horrible fake British accent. "When do the celebrations commence?"

He sounded *ridiculous*. But Shelby swallowed her laugh to avoid giving him away. She wasn't sure what would happen if they were found out, but she'd read of impalings, of torture devices like the wheel and the rack. *Lip balm, Shelby. Stay positive. Hot cocoa and sun salutations and reality TV. Focus on that.* They were going to get out of here. They had to.

The boy draped an arm adoringly around the girl's waist. "Anon. Tomorrow is the holiday."

The girl swept her hand across the marketplace. "But as you can see, most of the sweethearts have already arrived." She touched Shelby's shoulder playfully. "Don't forget to drop your name in Cupid's Urn before the sun sets!"

"Oh, right. You too," Shelby muttered awkwardly, like she always did when the people at the airport check-in counter told her to have a good trip. She bit the inside of her cheek as the girl and boy waved goodbye, arms still linked as they sauntered down the street.

Miles gripped her arm. "Isn't that *great*? A Valentine's fair!"

This, coming from a baseball-playing boy-next-door

whom Shelby once watched eat nine hot dogs in a single sitting. Since when did Miles get jazzed about a sappy Valentine's Day party?

She was about to say something sarcastic when she saw that Miles looked—well . . . hopeful. Like he actually wanted to go. *With her?* For some reason, she didn't want to crush him.

"Sure. Great." Shelby shrugged nonchalantly. "Sounds like fun."

"No." Miles shook his head. "I meant . . . the fallen angels are bound to be there, if they're going to be anywhere. That's where we'll find someone who will help us get home."

"Oh." Shelby cleared her throat. Of course that was what he meant. "Yeah, good point."

"What's wrong?" Miles dipped the ladle into the well and held the cool cup of water up to Shelby's lips. He stopped and wiped the edge clean with his sleeve, then held it out again.

Shelby felt herself blushing for no reason, so she closed her eyes and drank deeply, hoping she wouldn't catch some sort of withering sickness and die. After she'd finished, she said, "Nothing."

Miles dipped the ladle again and drank a big gulp, his eyes scanning the crowd.

"Look—" he said, dropping the ladle back into the bucket. He pointed behind Shelby to a raised platform at the edge of the market stalls where three girls were huddled together, doubled over in fits of giggles. Between them was a tall pewter pot with a fluted rim. It looked old as dirt and pretty ugly, the kind of expensive "artwork" Francesca might have in her office at Shoreline.

"That must be Cupid's Urn," Miles said.

"Oh, yes, obviously. Cupid's Urn." Shelby nodded sarcastically. "What the heck does that mean? Wouldn't Cupid have better taste?"

"It's a tradition carried over from the classical days of Rome," Miles said, going into scholarly mode as usual. Traveling with him was like carrying around an encyclopedia.

"Before Valentine's Day was Valentine's Day," he went on, his voice tinged with excitement, "it was called Lupercalia—"

"Looper—" She waved a hand, working out a bad pun. Then she saw Miles's expression. So earnest and sincere.

Registering her eyes on his face, he reached up instinctively to tug his baseball cap down over his eyes. His nervous habit. But his hands met only air.

He flinched as if embarrassed and tried to stuff his hand in his jeans pocket, but the coarse blue cloak covered his pants, so all he could do was cross his arms over his chest.

"You miss it, don't you?" Shelby asked.

"What?"

"Your hat."

"That old thing?" He shrugged too quickly. "Nah. Haven't even thought about it." He looked away, casting his eyes emptily around the square.

Shelby put her hand on his arm. "What were you saying about Looper . . . um, you know?"

His eyes flicked back to hers, dubious. "You really want to know?"

"Does the pope wear Prada?"

Now he smiled. "Lupercalia was really just a pagan celebration of fertility and the coming of spring. All the eligible women in the town would write their names on strips of parchment and drop them into the urn—like that one there. When the bachelors drew from the urn, whoever's name they pulled out would be their sweetheart for the year."

"That's barbaric!" Shelby cried. No way was some urn going to tell her who to go out with. She could make her own mistakes, thank you.

"I think it's sweet." Miles shrugged, looking away.

"You do?" Shelby's head swiveled back to him. "I mean, I guess it could be cool. But this urn tradition comes before the festival had anything to do with Saint Valentine, right?"

"Right," Miles said. "Eventually the church got

involved. They wanted to bring the pagan celebration under their control, so they attached a patron saint. They did that a lot with old holidays and traditions. Like it wasn't a threat if they owned it."

"Typical males."

"Now, in his life, the real Valentine was known as a defender of romance. People who couldn't legally get married—soldiers, for instance—came to him from all over and he'd perform the ceremony in secret."

Shelby shook her head. "How do you *know* all this stuff? Or rather, *why*?"

"Luce," Miles said, not meeting Shelby's eyes.

"Oh." Shelby felt like someone had just stuffed a stiff fist into her gut. "You learned about the history of Valentine's Day to impress *Luce*?" She kicked the dirt. "I guess some girls dig nerds."

"No, Shelby. I mean"—Miles gripped her shoulders and pivoted her to face the platform with the urn. "It's *Luce*. Right over there."

Luce wore a light brown dress with a wide skirt. Her long black hair was braided into three thick plaits, held together with narrow white ribbons. Her skin looked paler than usual, with a frosty pink flush dotting her cheekbones. She was circling the urn in slow, meditative steps, standing apart from the other girls. In the chaos of the square, Luce seemed to be the only person who was alone. Her eyes had that soft, unfocused look they got when she was in the trance of her thoughts.

"Shelby—wait!"

Shelby was already halfway across the square, almost running toward Luce, when Miles clasped a tight hand around her wrist. He pulled her to a stop, and she turned, ready to lay into him.

Except his expression . . . *glowed* with something Shelby couldn't decipher.

"You know this is the Lucinda of the past. This girl is not our friend. She won't *know* you—"

Shelby hadn't thought about that. She pretended she had. She turned and took another hard look at Lucinda. Her hair was dirty—not greasy, but something beyond greasy, really *dirty*—one thing Luce Price would never abide. Her clothes fit her strangely, from Shelby's modern standpoint, but Lucinda seemed comfortable in them. She seemed comfortable in everything, actually, which was also not very Luce Price. Shelby thought of Luce as chronically—though charmingly—maladjusted. It was one of the things she loved about Luce. But this girl? This girl seemed comfortable even in the desperate sadness saturating every movement she made. As if she was as accustomed to feeling glum as she was to the sun rising every day. Didn't she have friends to cheer her up? Wasn't that what friends were for?

"Miles," Shelby said, grasping his free wrist in her own hand and leaning close. "I know we agreed to let Daniel find our Lucinda Price, but this girl is *still* the Lucinda we care about . . . or an earlier version of her.

And the least we can do is cheer her up. Look how bummed she is. Look."

He bit his lip. "But—but—everything we've learned about Announcers says you shouldn't mess with—"

"Hiii there!" Shelby said in a singsong, pulling Miles along until they arrived at Lucinda's side. She didn't know where the Southern belle accent had come from, other than hearing present-day Luce's mom's drawl at Thanksgiving back in Georgia. And she had no idea what people here in this medieval British world would make of her sounding like a Georgia deb, but it was too late now.

A few feet behind her, Miles shook his head in horror. *It was an accident!* Shelby told him with her eyes.

Lucinda hadn't even noticed—that was how lost in sadness she was. Shelby had to step up right in front of her and wave a hand in her face.

"Oh," Lucinda said, blinking at Shelby with no hint of recognition. "Good day."

It shouldn't have hurt Shelby's feelings, but it did.

"H-haven't we met before?" Shelby stammered. "I think my cousin from, er, Windsor knows an uncle on your father's side of the family . . . or maybe it was the other way around."

"I'm sorry, I don't believe so, though perhaps—"

"You're Lucinda, right?"

Lucinda started, and for a moment there was a familiar spark in her eyes. "Yes."

Shelby pressed a hand to her heart. "I'm Shelby. This is Miles."

"Such unique names. You must have traveled from the North?"

"Sure." Shelby shrugged. "Very, very far north. So, we've never been to . . . ye olde Valentine's Faire here before. Are you dropping your name in the urn?"

"Me?" Lucinda swallowed, touching the hollow of her throat. "The idea that a stroke of chance could decide my heart's destiny does not appeal to me."

"Spoken like a girl who's got herself a studly boyfriend!" Shelby nudged Lucinda, forgetting they were strangers, forgetting that her words might be coarse and her sarcasm foreign to Lucinda's medieval sensibilities. "I mean . . . is there a knight you fancy, lady?"

"I was in love," Lucinda said somberly.

"Was?" Shelby repeated. "You mean *are* in love."

"I was. But he's gone."

"Daniel *left* you?" Miles was red in the face. "I mean—what was his name?"

But Lucinda didn't seem to have heard. "We met in the rose garden of his lord's castle. I must admit that I was trespassing, but I had seen so many fine ladies come and go, and the gate was open, and the flowers so, so comely—"

She clasped her hands to her heart and sighed with deep regret.

"That first day, he mistook me for a girl of higher

stature. Of class. I had my best kirtle on, my hair woven with hawthorn flowers, as some ladies do. It did look fine, but I fear it was dishonest."

"Oh, Lucinda," Shelby said. "I'm sure you're a lady in his eyes!"

"Daniel is a knight. He must marry a fitting lady. My family, we are common. My father is a free man, but he grows grain, just as his father did." She blinked and a tear slid down her cheek. "I never even told my love my name."

"If he loved you—and I'm sure he does—he'll know your true name," Miles said.

Lucinda shuddered as she took a breath. "Then, last week, as part of his knightly duty to the lord, he—he came by my father's door to gather eggs for the lord's Valentine feast. It was the anniversary of my christening. We were celebrating. To see my love's face when he saw me in our meager home . . . I tried to stop him going, but he took his leave without a word. I've looked for him in all our secret places—the hollowed oak tree in the forest, the northern fringe of the rose garden at dusk—but I have not seen him since."

Shelby and Miles shared a look. Obviously, Daniel didn't care about what kind of family Lucinda came from. It was the anniversary—the fact that she was getting closer to the limits of her curse—that had spooked him. By now Shelby was familiar with the way Daniel sometimes tried to pull away from Luce when he knew her death was near. He broke her heart to save her life. He was probably moping around somewhere, broken-hearted, too.

It had to be that way. This girl standing before Shelby had to die, maybe a hundred times before the lifetime when Shelby knew Luce—the lifetime when Luce got her first chance to break her curse.

It wasn't fair. It wasn't fair that she had to die again and again, and had to go through pain like this at so many moments in between. More than anyone, Lucinda deserved to be happy.

Shelby wanted to do something for Lucinda, even if it was something small.

She glanced at Miles again. He raised one eyebrow in a way Shelby hoped meant *Are you thinking what I'm thinking?* She nodded.

"This is only a big misunderstanding," Shelby said. "We know Daniel."

"You do?" Lucinda looked surprised.

"Tell you what: You go to the fair tomorrow, and I'm sure Daniel will be there, too, and you guys can just—"

Lucinda's lip quivered, and she buried her face in Shelby's shoulder as she began to weep. "I could not bear to see him draw another's name from the urn."

"Lucinda," Miles said so warmly that the girl's eyes

cleared and she looked at him in the intimate way Luce sometimes looked at him. It made Shelby strangely jealous. Shelby looked away as Miles asked, "You believe that Daniel truly loves you?"

Lucinda nodded.

"And in your heart," Miles went on, "do you really believe that the connection you have with Daniel is so weak that your family's position might sever the bond?"

"He—he does not have a choice. It is written in the Knights' Code. He must marry a—"

"Luce! Don't you know that your love is stronger than some dumb code?" Shelby blurted out.

Lucinda raised an eyebrow. "Come again?" she asked.

Miles shot Shelby a warning glance.

"I mean, erm . . . true love runs deeper and stronger than mere social niceties. If you love Daniel, then you must tell him how you feel."

"I feel odd." Lucinda was flushed, holding a hand over her breast. She closed her eyes, and for a moment Shelby thought she was going to burn up right then and there. Shelby took a step back.

But that wasn't how it worked, was it? Luce's curse had something to do with the way she and Daniel interacted, something his presence awakened in her.

"I want to believe that what you say is true. I do feel suddenly that our love is very strong."

"Strong enough that if we brought Daniel to you at the festival tomorrow," Shelby said, "you would go to him?"

Lucinda opened her eyes. They were wild and wide and brilliantly hazel. "I would go. I would go anywhere in the world to be with him again."

THREE

HIS SWORD, HIS WORD

"That was brilliant!" Shelby cried when Lucinda had gone and she and Miles were alone at the well.

In the western sky, the sun's rays had turned pale. Most of the citizens were making their way home, carts and satchels heavy with provisions for the evening's supper. Shelby hadn't eaten in a long time, but she hardly noticed the scents of roasting chicken and boiling potatoes in the air. She was running on the fumes of her excitement. "You and I were completely on the same page back there. It was like I thought something, and you said it—like a crazy rhythm we got into!"

"I know." Miles plunged the ladle into the bucket and took a long, slow drink of water. His freckles had come out in the sunlight. Shelby was still getting used to how different he looked without his baseball cap. "You were right—it felt good to make Luce feel better. Even if she's not *our* Luce." For a second, Miles's head jerked to the left, as if he'd heard something. His body stiffened.

"What is it?" Shelby asked.

But then his shoulders slumped a little lower than their normal casual mode. "Nothing. I thought I saw an Announcer, but it was nothing."

Shelby didn't want to think about Announcers; she was too excited. "You know what would be amazing?" she said, sitting down on the edge of the well. "We could go shopping for them both, get some lacy trinket for Luce and tell her it's from Daniel. I could write some cute poem—'roses are red' or whatever—hey, that'd probably be new to these medieval rubes. And we could—"

"Shelby?" Miles interrupted her. "What about getting home? We don't belong here, remember? We've already helped Lucinda by giving her hope to go to the Valentine's Faire, but we can't really do much else to change the way her curse plays out. We need to find an Announcer."

"Well, you know wherever Luce is, the rest of them are bound to be nearby," Shelby said quickly. "If we could just find Daniel, it would be, like, two birds, one stone. He'd go to the Faire; we'd find our way back to Shoreline."

"I don't know if it would be that easy to get Daniel to that Faire."

"Then we can't go home! Not until we make good on our promise to Luce! I don't want to be one more person who lets her down." Shelby felt suddenly deflated. "She deserves better."

Miles slowly exhaled. He paced around the well, brow furrowed—his thinking face. "You're right," he said finally. "What's one more day?"

"Really?" Shelby squealed.

"But where are we going to find Daniel? Didn't Lucinda say something about a castle?" Miles said. "We could find it and—"

"Knowing Daniel, he could be moping around anywhere. And I do mean *anywhere*."

Shelby heard the sound of horses' hooves and turned her head toward the wide central pathway through the marketplace. Past the merchants' stalls, which were being shut down for the evening, she caught a glimpse of a regal, snow-white horse.

When it passed the last merchant's awning and came into open view, Shelby gasped.

The figure in the black leather saddle lined with

ermine—whom Shelby, Miles, and most of the towns-people watched in unabashed awe—was truly a knight in shining armor.

Broad-shouldered, his identity obscured by his visor, the knight rode through the square with a commanding air of nobility. The riveted steel plates began at his feet, which were steadied in two stout stirrups. His legs were encased in polished greaves, and his mail coat was cut so close it clung to his muscular sides. His metal helmet had a flat top, with two curved plates meeting in an angled seal over his nose. There were tiny breathing holes in the front of the visor and a narrow slit across his eyes. It was alarming: He could see them, but they could only see the blinding outward evidence of him.

A sheath fastened at his left side carried a sword, and over his armor he wore a long white tunic with a red cross across the chest like one Shelby thought she'd seen in a Monty Python movie.

"Why don't we ask him?" Shelby said.

"Seriously?"

Shelby faltered. Sure, she was nervous about approaching a real live *knight*. But how else were they going to find Daniel?

"Do you have a better idea?" She pointed at the looming figure. "He's a knight. Daniel's a knight. Chances are they're gonna run in the same chivalric circle, right?"

"Okay, okay. And Shel?" Miles inhaled halfway,

something he did when he was nervous. Or when he thought he might be about to hurt Shelby's feelings. "Try not to use the Georgia peach accent, okay? It might have rolled right over love-struck Lucinda's head, but we need to be more careful about blending in. Remember what Roland said about messing with the past."

"I'm blending, I'm blending." Shelby hopped off the edge of the well, straightened her shoulders like she imagined a proper lady might do, gave Miles a wink that felt a little awkward, and strode toward the knight.

But she'd taken just two short strides when the knight turned to face her, lifted his visor, and narrowed his dark eyes into a glare—a glare that Shelby had earned several times before.

Speak of the devil. Hadn't Miles *just* mentioned Roland Sparks?

Roland glanced back and forth between Shelby and Miles. He clearly recognized them, which meant this was the Roland of their present-day era, their Roland, the one they'd last seen in Lucinda Price's battle-blasted backyard. Which meant they were in trouble.

"*What* are you two doing here?"

Miles was at Shelby's side instantly, his hands protectively around her shoulders. It was really decent of him, like he wasn't going to let her get busted alone. "We're looking for Daniel," he said. "Can you help us? Do you know where he is?"

"Help *you*? Find *Daniel*?" Roland gave them a baffled quirk of his dark eyebrows. "Don't you mean Luce, the mortal girl lost in her own Announcers? You kids are in way over your head."

"We know, we know, we don't belong here." Shelby put on her most repentant tone. "We got here by accident," she added, staring up at Roland on his incredible white horse. She'd had no idea horses were so huge. "We're trying to get home, but we're having trouble finding an Announcer—"

"Of course you are." Roland huffed. "Like I don't have enough obligations, now I've got to babysit, too." He raised a gloved hand casually. "I'll summon one for you."

"Wait." Miles stepped forward, interrupting Roland. "We thought, while we were here, we could maybe, um, do one nice thing for Lucinda. You know, the Lucinda of this era. Nothing major, just make her life a little brighter. Daniel ditched her—"

"You know how he gets sometimes—" Shelby cut in.

"Hold up. You saw Lucinda?" Roland asked.

"She was devastated," Miles said.

"And tomorrow is Valentine's Day," Shelby added.

The steed neighed, and Roland steadied it with the reins. "Was she cloven?"

Shelby wrinkled her nose. "Was she *what*?"

"Was she a union of her past and present selves?"

"You mean like—" Shelby was thinking of the way Daniel had looked in Jerusalem, lost and out of focus, like a 3-D movie with the glasses off.

But before she could answer, Miles's shoe crunched down on her toes. If Roland didn't like them being here, he sure wasn't going to like the fact that they'd been traveling around via the Announcers sort of everywhere. "Shhh," Miles whispered through the side of his mouth.

"Look, it's pretty simple: Did she recognize you?" Roland pressed.

Shelby sighed. "No."

"No," Miles said.

"Then she's the Luce of this time and we shouldn't interfere." Roland eyed them with frank suspicion but said no more. One of his long golden-black dreadlocks came loose from its elastic and tumbled from the recesses of his helmet. He tucked it away and looked around the city square, at the dogs attacking a snake of cow intestine, at the children kicking a lopsided leather ball through the muddy streets. He was clearly wishing he hadn't run into them.

"Please, Roland," Shelby said, reaching boldly for his chain-mail glove. *Gauntlet,* she thought. They're called *gauntlets.* "Don't you believe in love? Don't you have a heart?"

Shelby felt the words hanging in the frosty air and wished she could take them back. Surely she'd gone too far. She didn't know what Roland's story was. He'd sided with Lucifer when the angels fell, but he'd never seemed all that bad. Just cryptic and inscrutable.

He opened his mouth to say something, and Shelby waited to hear yet another lecture about the dangers of Announcer travel, or to be threatened with being turned in to Francesca and Steven at Roland's whim. She winced and looked away.

Then she heard the soft clank of a visor being shut.

When she looked up, Roland's face was hidden again. The visor's dark eye slit was unreadable.

Way to ruin things, Shelby.

"I will find Daniel for you." Roland's voice boomed from behind the visor, making Shelby jump. "I will see that he arrives in time for tomorrow's Faire. I have one final errand to attend to, and then I will be back here to provide you both with an Announcer that will spirit you back to Shoreline, where you should be now. I want no arguments. Take my offer or leave it."

Shelby clenched her jaw to keep it from dropping open. He was going to help them.

"No—no arguments," Miles stammered. "That will be fine, Roland. Thank you."

Then came a slight dip of Roland's helmet, which Shelby took to be a nod, but he said nothing else. He only nudged his white horse around to face the path that led back out of the city. Merchants scattered as the animal trotted, then broke into a gallop, its white tail streaming behind it like a disappearing puff of smoke.

Shelby noticed something strange: Instead of riding proudly out of town, Roland sat with head lowered, his shoulders a bit slumped. As if something inexplicable had changed his mood. Was it something she'd said?

"That was intense," Miles said, standing next to her.

Shelby inched closer to him, so that their arms were touching, and it made her feel better.

Roland was going to find Daniel. He was going to help them.

Shelby found herself smiling a very un-Shelby-like smile. Somewhere under all that armor, maybe there was a heart that believed in the power of true love.

For all her outward cynicism, Shelby had to admit that she too believed in love. And she could tell by the way Miles had consoled Lucinda this afternoon that he was a believer, too. Together they watched the glow of twilight's sun on Roland's armor and listened to the clatter of hooves on cobblestone tapering into silence.

FOUR

HAND IN GLOVE

One thing about the Middle Ages: The stars were unbelievable.

Unbothered by city lights, the sky was a glittering landscape of galaxies, the kind of sky that made Shelby want to lie awake a long time and stare. Just before dusk, the sun had finally burned through the gray winter clouds, and now the dark canvas above was awash with stars.

"That's the Big Dipper, isn't it?" Miles asked, pointing up at a bright arc in the sky.

"Beats me." Shelby shrugged, though she leaned in to follow his finger with her eyes. She could smell his skin, familiar and a little citrusy. "I didn't know you were into astronomy."

"I didn't, either. Never have been. But there's something about the stars tonight . . . or something about tonight in general. Everything feels kind of noteworthy. You know?"

"Yeah," Shelby breathed, lost in the heavens she'd never thought too much about. She felt close to them in a weird way. Close to Miles, too. "I know."

Once they'd agreed to stay on another night, scrappy Shelby had procured a blanket and some rope and— using skills learned during her days on Skid Row— fashioned them into an almost elegant tent. Like so many of the visiting revelers, she and Miles had set up camp on a high slope of the green outside the city walls. Miles had even found firewood, though neither one of them knew how to start a fire without a match.

It was kinda nice here, actually. Yeah, there were crazy coyote noises coming from the woods, but Shelby reminded herself that sometimes nights at Shoreline carried the same shrill cries. She and Miles would just stick together—and hide behind some meaty medieval people if any wild creatures came poking out of the forest.

A special holiday night market was setting up near the road, so after pitching the tent, they'd split up, with a plan for Miles to find some food and Shelby to hunt for Valentine's Day gifts to give to Luce and Daniel the next day. Then they would meet back at camp to dine under the stars.

In the hour before sunset, the vendors in the city had moved the party outside. The night market was different from the daytime market inside the walls, which had sold everyday items like cloth and grain. The night market, Shelby realized, was a special-occasion affair, just for the Valentine's holiday when the city overflowed with far-traveling merchants and other visitors.

The green was crowded with newly pitched tents, many of which doubled as bartering centers. Shelby didn't have much to offer, but she managed to exchange her hot-pink elastic hair band for a lace doily in the shape of a heart, which she planned to give to Luce "from Daniel."

She'd also happily swapped a hemp ankle bracelet Phil had given her on some date back at Shoreline for a leather dagger sheath she figured Daniel might like. Guys were hard to shop for.

The hair band and the anklet were less than worthless to Shelby, but they were exotic to the merchants. "What is this alchemical substance that stretches and retains its shape?" they asked her, examining the band as if it were a priceless gem. Shelby had stifled her laughter, those medieval torture devices never too far from her thoughts.

Like always after shopping, Shelby was ravenous.

She hoped Miles had dug up some good grub. She was hurrying across the crowded green to meet him when a blurry thought came into focus: What was she forgetting?

"Oh, what a lovely bonnet!" A fair-haired woman with a broad smile appeared before her. She stroked the lace veil of the wimple that Shelby had swiped from the cart that morning. "Is it one of Master Tailor's?"

"Uh, who?" Shelby's guilty blush crept up to the tips of her stolen hat.

"His stall's just over yonder." The woman pointed at a tent made of stiff white canvas about ten feet away. "Henry's got three sisters, all gorgeous seamstresses. Most of the year, their needles fly only for the vestments of the church's mystery plays, but the girls always manage something small and special for the Faire. Their work takes my breath away."

The tent's flaps were open, and there, under an awning, stood the stout man whose cart she and Miles had tried to hop like a freight train that morning. The man who had swiped Miles's hat. A small crowd had gathered and was giving off oohs and aahs, admiring something apparently very precious. Shelby had to press up against the other fairgoers before she recognized the item drawing so many hungry eyes:

A bright blue Dodgers cap.

"Admire the exquisite dye of this buckram visor!"

Henry Tailor was deep in the throes of his sales pitch, as if the hat had always been a part of his collection, as if he had sewn it himself. "Have you ever seen such stitches? Impeccably regular, to the point of . . . invisibility!"

"And when a sword slices through that felt, Henry, what then?" a man jeered. The crowd began to buzz that perhaps the visor was not the most invincible item in Henry's collection.

"Fools," Henry said. "This visor is not armor, but a thing of beauty. Is it not possible that a thing can be made simply to please the eye and the heart?"

As the fairgoers hooted, Shelby's heart hammered in her chest, because she knew what she had to do.

"I'll buy the hat!" she shouted suddenly.

"It's not for sale!" Henry said.

"Of course it's for sale," Shelby said, pushing aside her nerves about her awful English accent, pushing aside a few startled people, pushing aside everything but her need to get the hat. It was important to Miles, and Miles was important to her. "Here," she cried, "take my bonnet in exchange! My, um, father bought it for me this morning and it doesn't, um, fit."

Henry looked up, and Shelby had a moment of panic—certainly he would know she'd stolen the bonnet. Only, when he tilted his head at Shelby, he didn't even seem to register that the hat had once belonged to him. "Yes, that bonnet does make your ears stick out. But that's not enough."

What? She didn't have big ears! Shelby was about to give Henry a piece of her mind when she remembered what was important here.

"Come now! That hat is old, its material faded!" She pointed an accusing finger. "And what manner of wickedness do those letters emblazoned on the front signify?"

"Are they letters?" someone in the crowd asked.

"I don't know how to read," said another.

And it was clear Henry didn't read, either. "What do they say?" he asked. "I thought they were mere ornamentation." And then, remembering that he'd claimed to have made the hat, he added, "The design was given to me by a passing gentleman."

"They are the mark of the devil!" Shelby improvised, her voice getting louder as she gained confidence. "The spiky arms are his mark and his brand."

The crowd gasped and pushed closer. The smell of them made Shelby feel like she couldn't get a breath.

Henry held the cap away from him. "Is that so? Then why do you want it?"

"Why do you think? I aim to destroy it in the name of all that is holy and right in the world."

There was a murmur of approval from the crowd.

"I will burn it and rid this world of its evil mark!" She was really getting into this.

A few in the crowd gave feeble cheers.

"I will protect us all from the bane of the cap!"

Henry scratched his head. "It's just a cap, though, innit?"

Around Shelby, people turned to look at her. "Well, yes, but . . . my point is that I'll take it off your hands."

Tailor looked at the bonnet in her hand, his left eyebrow rising. "That handiwork looks familiar," he muttered. Then he looked again at Miles's cap. "An even trade, then?"

Shelby held out the lacy wimple. "An even trade."

The man nodded and the exchange was made. Miles's treasured Dodgers cap felt like solid gold in Shelby's hands, and she couldn't get back to the tent fast enough. He was going to be so happy! She bounded up the green, past minstrels singing sad and lonely songs, past children in the eternal game of tag, and soon she saw the outline of Miles's shoulders in the dark.

Only, it wasn't dark.

Miles had figured out how to make a fire! And he was roasting a forkful of sausages over the open flame. When he looked up at her and smiled, a tiny dimple she'd never noticed before appeared in his left cheek. Shelby felt dizzy. It might have been from running all that way. Or the sudden heat of the fire.

"Hungry?" Miles asked.

She nodded, too nervous about her news of having

reclaimed his cap to find words. She held the hat behind her back, self-conscious about everything. Her posture, the gift, her baggy medieval clothes. But this was Miles; he wouldn't judge her. Then why did she suddenly feel so jittery?

"Thought you might be. Hey, where's your bonnet?"

Was there a hint of regret in his voice? Did her hair look ridiculous? Now she didn't even have the elastic band to pull it back.

She flushed. "I traded it."

"Oh. For something to give to Luce and Daniel?"

The way the light played off his face, Miles looked like her best friend and also like an entirely new person. Someone, she realized, she would very much like to get to know.

"Yeah." Shelby felt weird, standing over him with her crazy lion's mane. Why didn't she have hair like Luce, hair that was smooth and shiny and sexy and stuff? Hair that boys liked. Miles had liked Luce's hair. He was still staring at Shelby. "What?"

"No big deal. Sit down. There's cider, and some bread."

Shelby dropped onto the grass next to Miles, careful to hide his cap in the folds of her dress. She wanted to give it to him at the right moment, like after her stomach stopped growling. He slid a sizzling sausage onto a thick, crusty slice of bread and handed her a dented tin cup of cider. They clinked cups, locked eyes.

"Where'd you get all this stuff?"

"You think you're the only one who can barter? I had to say goodbye to two good shoelaces for that sandwich, lady, so eat up."

As Shelby took a bite and sipped her drink, she was glad to see that Miles wasn't staring at her hair. He was gazing at the expanse of tents leading up to the city, at the smoke of a hundred campfires commingling in the air. She felt warmer and happier than she had in a very long time.

Finishing his sandwich before Shelby had even taken a second bite, Miles swallowed. "You know, this Luce-and-Daniel saga, their impossible love, the unbreakable curse, fate and destiny and all that . . . when we first started learning about it in classes, and even when I met Luce, it sounded like—"

"A bunch of hooey?" Shelby cut in. "That's what I thought, anyway."

"Well, yeah," Miles admitted. "But recently, going through the Announcers with you, really seeing how much more there is to this world, meeting Daniel in Jerusalem, watching how different Cam was when he was engaged . . . Maybe there is such a thing as true love."

"Yeah." Shelby mulled that over, chewing. "Yeah."

Out of nowhere, she wanted very badly to ask Miles something. But she was scared. And not the scared of having to sleep outside in an animal-filled forest, or the scared of being far, far away from home without any certainty you'd find your way back again. This was a raw and vulnerable kind of scared, whose intensity made her tremble.

But if she didn't ask, she'd never know. And that'd be worse.

"Miles?"

"Yeah?"

"Have you ever been in love?"

Miles plucked a brown blade of grass and twirled it between his palms. He flashed her a grin, then gave an embarrassed laugh. "I don't know. I mean . . . probably not." He coughed. "Have you?"

"No," she said. "Not even close."

Neither one seemed to know what to say after that. For a while, they just sat in nervous silence. Sometimes Shelby forgot that it was nervous silence, and it felt like comfortable silence with her friend Miles. But then she'd sneak a look at him, and catch him looking at her, and his eyes would be all magical blue, and everything felt really different, and she'd get nervous again.

"Ever wish you'd lived in another era?" Miles finally changed the subject, and it felt like someone had popped a huge balloon of tension. "I could get into wearing armor, being chivalrous, all that."

"You would make a great knight! Not me, though, I stick out like a sore thumb here. I like my noise in California."

"Me too. Hey, Shel?" His eyes pored over her. She felt hot even as a gust of February wind bit through her rough wool dress. "Do you think it's going to be different when we get back to Shoreline?"

"Of course it's going to be different." Shelby looked down and plucked at the grass. "I mean, we'll be sitting in the mess hall reading the *Tribune* and plotting pranks to play on the non-Nephilim. We won't be, like, drinking from medieval wells and stuff."

"That's not what I mean." Miles turned to face her. He drew her chin up with his finger. "I mean you and me. We're different here. I like the way we are here." A pause. A deep blue gaze. "Do you?"

Shelby had known that wasn't what he meant. But she was scared to talk about what else he might mean. Because what if she got it wrong? However she and Miles "were" here, she liked it, a lot. All day she'd been feeling this *buzz* around him. But she couldn't express it. It made her tongue-tied.

Why couldn't he just read her mind? (Not that it was any less confusing in there.) But no, Miles was hanging on her answer, which was overdue, and simple, and also really, really complicated.

"Sure." Shelby was blushing. She needed a distraction. She reached for the baseball cap. That way he'd stare at it instead of her red cheeks.

"The reason I asked about your bonnet," Miles said

before she could give him the cap, "is because I found these in the market tonight." He held up a pair of buff leather gloves with white tabbed cuffs. They were beautiful.

"You bought those? For me?"

"Traded for them, actually. You should have seen how much the glove maker flipped over a little pack of gum." He smiled. "Anyway, your hands were so cold all day, and I thought they'd match your bonnet."

Shelby couldn't help it. She started cracking up. She doubled over and banged on the ground and hooted. It felt so good to let go of all that pent-up nervous energy, to release it into the Valentine's Eve air and just laugh.

"You hate them." Miles sounded crestfallen. "I know they're not your normal style, but they were the same color as that bonnet and—"

"No, Miles, that's not it." Shelby sat back up and sobered when she saw his face. Then she started laughing again. "I traded the bonnet to get you this." She held up the Dodgers cap.

"No way." He reached for it with the air of a kid who couldn't believe that the presents under the Christmas tree were really his.

Silently, Shelby held the gloves in her hands. Miles gripped the cap in his. After a long moment, they tried their gifts on.

With the cap tugged tightly over his blue eyes, Miles

looked like his old self again, the boy Shelby recognized from a hundred lectures at Shoreline, the boy she'd first stepped through the Announcers with, the boy who was, she realized, her closest friend.

And the gloves—the gloves were amazing. The softest leather, the most delicate design. They fit her perfectly, almost like Miles knew the exact shape of her hands. She looked up to thank him, but his expression made her pause.

"What's wrong?"

Miles scratched his forehead. "I dunno. Would you mind, actually, if I took the cap off? I realized today I could see you better without it, and I liked it that way."

"See me?" Shelby didn't know why, of all times, her voice chose that moment to crack.

"Yeah. You." He took her hands. Her pulse picked up. Everything about that moment felt really important.

There was just one thing that was wrong.

"Miles?"

"Yeah?"

"Do you mind if I take the gloves off? I love them, and I will wear them, I promise, but right now, I—I can't feel your hands."

Ever so gently, Miles tugged off the leather gloves, one finger at a time. When he was finished, he laid them on the ground and took both of her hands in his again. Strong and reassuring and somehow totally surprising,

Miles's grip made her grin from the inside out. In the bough of the laurel tree behind them, a nightingale trilled sweetly. Shelby swallowed. Miles took a slow breath.

"Do you know what I thought when Roland said he was going to send us home tomorrow?"

Shelby shook her head.

"I thought: *Now I get to spend Valentine's Day in this incredibly romantic place with this girl I really like.*"

Shelby didn't know what to say. "You're not talking about Luce, are you?"

"No." He watched her eyes, waiting for something. Shelby felt that dizziness again. "I'm talking about you."

In her seventeen years, Shelby had been kissed by a lot of frogs and a few toads. And every time it got to this moment, the boy would always make the ultimate loser gesture, saying, "Can I kiss you now?" She knew some girls thought that was polite, but to Shelby, it was just a huge pain in the butt. She always ended up saying something sarcastic back, and it always just annihilated the mood. She was terrified that Miles was going to ask if he could kiss her. She was terrified he *wasn't* going to ask if he could kiss her.

Luckily, Miles didn't leave her too much time for terror.

He leaned in very slowly and cupped her cheek in the palm of his hand. His eyes were the color of the starry sky above them. When he guided her chin closer to his, tilting her face ever so slightly, Shelby closed her eyes.

Their lips connected in the sweetest kiss.

Simple, a few soft pecks. Nothing too complicated; they were just starting out, after all. When Shelby opened her eyes and saw the look in his—the smile she knew as well as her own—she knew she'd been given the best Valentine's Day gift there was. She wouldn't have traded it for the world.

LOVE LESSONS

THE VALENTINE OF ROLAND

ONE

THE LONG AND
BLINDING ROAD

Roland rode hard for the city's northern gates. Though his route would take him past the scene of the worst moment of his life, he did not detour. He was on a mission.

His horse, a stranger to him until a few hours ago—when he'd lifted her from the lord's stables—adapted intuitively to his needs. She was a snow-white Arabian who looked fine in her black leather knight's tack. Before Roland had found her, he'd had his eye on a dappled plowman's horse with ample flanks—a working horse could travel longer than a nobleman's horse, and on less feed—but Roland didn't feel right stealing from the peasant class.

This one—he was calling her Blackie after the single dark splash on her nose—had whinnied and reared when he first mounted her, but after a few discreet turns around the muddy path near the sheepfolds, they were friends. He had always had a knack with animals, especially horses. Animals could hear the music in his voice more clearly than humans. Roland could whisper a few words to a startled filly and calm her like sunshine after a tornado.

By the time Roland passed through the mayhem of the marketplace, horse and rider were a seamless partnership, which was more than he could say for his armor. The set he'd nicked from the lord's son's armaments chamber in the castle did not fit him. It was long in the leg and narrow in the chest and it stank of sour perspiration. None of these qualities agreed with Roland, whose body was accustomed to an *haute*r couture.

As he clipped past the gates, careful to skirt the lord's line of sight, Roland had simply ignored the citizens' alarmed looks and their conjecturing murmurs about what battle he was riding into. This formal armor—with its damned mail vest, girded with a twenty-pound embellished belt, and the stifling steel helmet that wouldn't sit straight because of his dreadlocks—was worn solely for fighting; it was too conspicuous and cumbersome for casual travel. He knew that. He felt it absolutely with every shuddering stride of his horse.

But this suit was the only thing Roland could find that would obscure his identity to the extent that he required. He hadn't come all this way to be bothered with mortals attempting to seize and imprison a demon they mistook for a Moor.

He needed a disguise that would not hinder his attainment of one goal: keeping Daniel's medieval past self out of trouble.

Not Lucinda. Daniel.

Lucinda Price, Roland believed, knew what she was doing. And even when she had no idea what she was doing, she always did the right thing. It was impressive. The angels who followed Luce into the Announcers—Gabbe, Cam, even Arriane—did not give Luce enough credit. But Roland had first noticed a change in her at Sword & Cross—a strange heedless certainty that she'd never possessed in any of her earlier lives, as if she had finally glimpsed the depths of her old soul. Luce might not have known what she was doing when she stepped through on her own, but Roland knew she would figure everything out. This was the endgame, and she needed to play her part.

That was why it was Daniel who worried Roland.

It would be just like Daniel to blunder into Luce and

ruin everything. Someone needed to make sure he didn't do anything stupid, which was why Roland had followed him through the Announcers in Luce's backyard.

But finding Daniel had been harder than he expected. Roland had been too late in Helston, just missed him at the Bastille, and likely wouldn't catch him here, either. If he were being smart, Roland would just skip out and try to intercept Daniel in one of their earlier lives.

If he were being smart.

But then he'd spotted the two unchaperoned Anachronisms baldly scheming at the well—in broad daylight, in the center of the city, in their bad clothes and worse accents.

Did they know nothing?

Roland liked the Nephilim well enough. Shelby was a solid, decent kind of person, and not bad to look at. And Miles—he had a reputation for getting too close to Luce at Shoreline, but . . . wouldn't any guy in Miles's shoes have tried? Give the kid a break, was Roland's gloss. Miles was all golden heart and very little badass.

Roland understood that the Nephilim kids were here out of pure goodwill. They had a soft spot for their friend Luce. And it was clear that Shelby and Miles had high hopes for romance at the Valentine's Day Faire— for Luce and Daniel, and maybe even for themselves.

They probably don't know that yet, Roland thought, and grinned.

Mortals could rarely recognize their true feelings before those true feelings hit them in the face.

It happened this way for many couples who spent time basking in the glow of Daniel and Lucinda. Roland had witnessed it before. Daniel and Lucinda were emblems of romance, ideals that every mortal and some immortals needed to believe in, whether or not they themselves were capable of making a connection so true. Daniel and Lucinda were an idea that informed the way the rest of the world fell in love.

It was a powerful spell under which to find oneself.

Of course, Roland had to razz the Nephilim for stepping through into one of Lucinda's medieval lives. They should be where they belonged, in their own time, where their actions wouldn't cause any historic catastrophes.

So he'd chewed them out a little. It would keep them in line until he returned to escort them safely home. Traveling with them was the only way he could ensure that they wouldn't wind up somewhere even farther away from Shoreline.

But first? He could indulge them. Track down Daniel and make sure he got his sullen self to the Valentine's Faire. Giving Daniel and Luce a moment of happiness was no sweat off Roland's back, and besides, it gave him something to do.

And in this particular era, Roland needed something to do.

To keep his mind off other things.

In the cold February gloom, Roland rode past a glebe, where serf-tended crops padded the pockets of the local clergymen. He rode past a Gothic church, with its pointed arches and thorny spires. *God's house.* He couldn't stop the thought from entering his mind. It had been a long time since he'd been in one of those. He crossed a high bridge over the swollen, muddy river, and turned his horse toward the knights' stronghold he knew was about a half day's ride to the north.

It was not a pleasant journey: rough road and ugly weather. Blackie kicked up high splashes of mud, painting her flanks a dingy gray-brown. And the cold caused the hinges of Roland's armor to stiffen into near-immobility.

Still, in most ways, there was something sweet in returning to this past. A romantic like Daniel might say chivalry had never really died, but then, Daniel had a complicated relationship with both love and death. Roland had lived among this early brand of chivalry for years. It was nearly over now in the Middle Ages, and it was certainly dead in the present tense Roland had just traveled from. There was no question in his mind.

But once upon a time . . .

For the briefest moment he remembered a glimmer of golden hair streaming in the wind.

He flipped up the visor of his helmet and gasped for

air. He would not think of her. That was not why he was here.

He nudged Blackie forward and shook his head, trying to clear his mind.

Roland was less than a mile from the band of knights he was seeking. He scanned the horizon: the sweeping dip of vales to the east, a rainstorm behind him and to the west. Ahead, the road wound up and around through twists of hills that formed a protective barrier for the city. Also ahead stood a castle that he intended to avoid. He would ride a wide berth around it. And on the other side of that castle was the road—if it was still in passable condition—that would lead him straight to the Daniel of this era. And to his own medieval self.

In his long-ago memory of this era, he remembered how the strangely clad knight had appeared before them, bearing orders from the king.

The knight had slowed his horse at the threshold of their tents and had passed around a decree commanding the men to abandon their post for two nights to celebrate the new St. Valentine's holy day, as was God's will. Only a few of them could read, so most of the men took the good news on faith. Roland still remembered the whoops and hollers that came from his fellow knights.

The knight had not spoken a word—had simply delivered the decree and galloped away . . . on his coal-black horse.

Strange. Roland looked down at Blackie, stroked her silver-white mane.

If this was Roland's destiny—to be the angel behind the visor who gave Daniel a Valentine's Day gift, directing him back to the arms of the girl he loved—then some event would have to transpire that would allow him to swap his white horse for a black one. And someone would have to place a king's decree in his hand.

Stranger things happened, he knew, nearly every day.

He put his heels to Blackie's flanks and rode on, sweating one moment, shivering the next.

❊

Eventually, Roland rode right up to the castle. It guarded the northernmost fief in the county, the last outpost on the way to the knights' camp. He sat astride his mount for a moment, taking in the familiar stonework.

The castle towered before him like a colossus. There were chalk-white chimneys over each chamber, narrow slits to afford a view from each façade. Corbels and cornices decorated the dark-gray blocks of stone, whose magnitude made Roland feel small. The castle's size boggled his mind. It always had, even for that brief stretch of time when he had passed through its gates nearly every day—and climbed its grooved stones to reach a single balcony every night.

His knees shook against his horse's flanks. His heart felt as if it had swelled to ten times its natural size. It beat as if every palpitation might be its last. The backs of his shoulders burned, and he wanted to fly far away, but his wings were encased in the full metal jacket on his back and he would not take it off.

Besides, no matter how far Roland flew, he could not escape the terror spreading through his soul.

Inside this castle lived a girl named Rosaline. She was the only being in the universe Roland had ever truly loved.

TWO

CRUMBLING WALLS

Blackie neighed softly as Roland slipped off her back. He led her to a budless apple tree at the southern limits of Rosaline's father's property and tied her bridle around the trunk.

How many times had Roland circled the trees in this orchard, carrying his love's wide woven basket on his arm, trailing behind her, adoring her slow movements as she plucked red fruit from the branches?

Her father was an earl or a duke or a baron or some other variety of greedy land magnate. Roland had stopped caring about such mortal titles after a thousand years of having to watch their kind play at war games. This mortal's sole passion in life seemed to be exactly that: waging war and stealing the riches of nearby fiefdoms and making life a living hell for all his neighbors. The band of knights Daniel and Roland served with fell under his sway, so Roland and his fellows had spent many hours outside and within these castle walls.

He dug into Blackie's saddlebags and found a dried apple, then fed it to the horse while he took the measure of the situation.

He remembered this Valentine's Day Faire. He knew that it took place after his affair with Rosaline had ended. Their love would have been over for . . . five years by now.

He shouldn't have stopped here. He should have known this would happen—that the memories would flood his mind and cripple him.

Not a day went by, these thousand years, that Roland did not regret the way he had ended things with Rosaline. He had designed his life around that regret: walls and walls and walls, each one with its own impenetrable façade. The regret formed a castle inside him many universes vaster than the one that stood before him now. Perhaps that was why this English castle's size moved him so dramatically—it reminded Roland of the fortress within him.

He was far too late to redeem himself with her.

And yet . . .

He gave Blackie an encouraging scratch and made for the castle. There was a stone-flagged walkway lined with hibernating primrose bushes, which ended at a heavy metal gate. Roland avoided this and took a side path. He walked under the tree line of the bordering woods until he could slink along out of sight in the shadow of the castle's western wall. It towered over him, rising fifty feet in the air before the first window offered a glimpse out.

Or in.

Rosaline used to wait for him there, her blond hair trailing over the window's edge. It was the signal that she was alone—and awaiting Roland's lips. The window was empty now, and to gaze upon it from the ground below gave Roland a rusty feeling of homesickness, as if he were very, very far from the place where he belonged.

No guards looked down from the battlements here, he knew. The wall was too high. He left the shadows and walked over to stand directly beneath the window.

He ran his hands along the wall, remembering the grooves his feet had found so many times before. He'd never dared then to unleash his wings in front of Rosaline. It was enough to ask a mortal like her to love him despite the color she perceived in his skin. Her father never saw Roland without his visor, and would not have permitted a Moor to fight for him.

Roland could have changed the way he looked; angels did it all the time. How often had Daniel changed his mortal guise for Luce? They'd all stopped counting.

But it wasn't Roland's style to follow trends. He was a classicist. His soul felt comfortable—as comfortable as was possible—in this particular skin. There were occasions, like today, when his looks caused some dull hassle, but it was never anything Roland couldn't withstand. Rosaline said she loved him for who he was inside. And he loved her for that openness . . . but she didn't *really* know. There were still some things about himself Roland knew he could never expose.

He would not expose himself now, not by shedding his armor or baring his wings. Habit would help him scale the wall the old-fashioned way.

The path within the walls came back to him, as if it were illuminated by the same golden sheen his exposed wings cast upon the world.

Roland began to climb.

At first, he was cautious in his ascent, but even in the creaky metal armor, he soon felt nimble again with light memories of love.

A few short minutes later, he reached the top of the outer wall and heaved his legs onto the narrow ledge of the parapet. Righting himself, he slunk along to the far turret and gazed up at its conical sienna spire. From there, it was a treacherous climb up to the ring of arched windows circling the tower. But he knew that there was a narrow terrace outside one of the windows, and a fine lip of stone encircling the tower. He could stand upon it and peer inside.

Soon enough, he arrived at the ledge and clung firmly to the stonework alongside the window. That was when he noticed the open balcony door. A red silk curtain billowed in the wind. And there, beyond it, a brush of mortal movement. Roland held his breath.

Blond waves of hair, long and loose, hung down the back of a glorious green dress. Was it her? It had to be.

He longed to reach in and pull her from the window, to make the world the way it used to be. His fingers grew numb from his hard grip on the ledge, and in the pivotal moment when the golden-haired goddess spun around, Roland froze so quickly, so completely, he thought he would tumble like an icicle to the ground.

He pulled himself away and back onto the ledge, his chest flat against the wall, but he could not pull his eyes away from the girl.

It was not her.

This was Celia, the lord's younger daughter. She must have been sixteen now—Rosaline's age when Roland had broken her heart. She resembled her sister: fair skin, blue eyes, rose-petal lips, and all that stunning flaxen hair. But the fire within her—that mighty conflagration that Roland had adored in Rosaline—was a dying ember in Celia.

Still, Roland was riveted, unable to make the slightest move. If Celia swept out through the window and onto the balcony, as she looked like she was about to do, Roland would be caught.

"Sister?"

That voice—like a stringed instrument, only richer. Rosaline!

For a fraction of a second, Roland saw a shadow in the doorway, and then: the clean, graceful profile of the only girl he'd ever loved. His heart stopped. He could not breathe. He wanted to cry out her name, to reach for her—

But his sweating palms betrayed him and his grip faltered. For several eternal seconds, Roland felt like he was hovering in the air—and then he plummeted six long stories to the muddy ground.

❊

A memory:

The open doors of a dilapidated barn.

Roland recognized it as the rickety structure on the northeast corner of the castle grounds. The sun swept past the doorway at about six o'clock on summer evenings, so Roland guessed by the golden light on the hay that it was nearly seven. Nearly suppertime—or the ever-too-brief stretch when Roland could persuade Rosaline to steal a few moments alone with him.

Through the wide wooden doors he saw two

silhouettes huddled in a dark back corner. There, between the chicken feed and a rusty pile of sickles, Roland saw his earlier self.

He barely recognized the boy he'd been. They were one and the same, and yet something made this boy actually look young. Hopeful. Unspoiled. His woolen tunic hugged his body, and his eyes were as bright as a newborn filly's. *She* did that to him—stripped away millennia spent toiling on Earth, his entire existence in Heaven, and the weighty Fall afterward.

He might have been experienced at war, at rebellion against the divine, but when it came to romance, Roland's heart had been the heart of a child.

He sat on a three-legged wooden stool and gazed—so earnestly it embarrassed him to recall it—at the gorgeous blond-haired girl before him.

Rosaline reclined on her side in the hay, oblivious to the thistles that clung to her satin gown. Her hair had a luster that was lovelier even than he remembered, and her skin was as smooth and bright as fresh-skimmed cream. Her downward gaze meant that all Roland could see of her fair blue eyes was the soft curtain of lashes drifting over them. In those days, her full lips had two expressions: the pout they clung to now and the brief gift of a smile she sometimes bestowed on Roland. Both were desirable. Both did strange things to him.

She shifted in the hay, feigning boredom but feigning

it poorly. She was transfixed by his every movement, he could see that now.

"I do have one more trifle. Should my lady like to hear it?" his past self said.

Roland recalled the eager tilting of his past self's chin and burned with shame. Now he remembered why she had taken so much convincing to agree to meet him in the barn.

All he did was assault her with bad poetry.

The boy on the stool did not wait—he clearly *could* not wait—for Rosaline's ladylike groan. And when Roland launched into his gruesome verse, no one would ever have guessed that this failed sonneteer had once been the Angel of Music.

"Snowy peaks are sub-sublime,
Compared to dazzling Rosaline.
Soft-eyed kittens are unkind,
In the lap of Rosaline.
As a poem's made of lines,
So am I of Rosaline.
They that toil to sheaf and bind,
Then to cart with Rosaline.
As the nut transcends the rind,
Such a nut is Rosaline.
He that mysteries would find,
First must eyeball Rosaline."

At the end, Roland looked up to see Rosaline's face pinched into a frown. He remembered it now, struggled to endure it a second time, and felt the same heaviness in his stomach, like an anvil falling off a cliff.

She said: "Why do you infect me with such clumsy verse?"

This time, in his memory, Roland heard it in her voice: Of course! She was *teasing* him.

He should have known it when she reached for his hand and drew him down onto the hay with her. His heart had been hammering too loudly for him to hear her implication, which now, clearly, was *Shut up and kiss me*.

And how he had kissed her!

That first time their lips connected, something ignited within Roland, as if his soul had been electrified. His body had gone rigid with the effort of trying not to mess a single thing up. His lips were welded to hers, but limply. His hands were two claws glued to her shoulders. Rosaline writhed against his grip, but for the life of him he could not move.

At last she let out a sweet giggle and snaked free from his arms. She leaned backward in the hay, her pink lips pursed and off-limits once again. She eyed him the way a child eyes an out-of-favor toy. "That lacked grace."

Roland lurched forward on his knees, his hands

planted in the rough hay. "Shall I try again? I am certain I can do better—"

"Well, I should hope so." Her laugh was coy and elegant. She leaned away just long enough to tease him, then lay back in the hay and closed her eyes. "You may try again."

Roland inhaled deeply, drinking in the sweetness of every part of her. But just as he was about to bestow another awkward kiss, Rosaline pressed a hand against his chest.

She must have felt his heart race, but she didn't let on.

"This time," she instructed, "not so stilted. More . . . *fluidity*. Think of the flow of a poem. Well, perhaps not *your* poems. Perhaps your favorite poem by another. Throw yourself into my kiss."

"Like this?" Roland all but fell on top of her, rolling to the side and finding himself facefirst in the hay. He turned toward her, flushed.

Side by side they lay, facing one another. She took his hands. Their hips were touching through their clothes. The tips of their feet kissed without embarrassment. Her face was inches away from his.

"You missed my mouth." Her lips parted in an alluring smile. "Roland, love means not being afraid to let yourself go, trusting that I will desire everything you have to offer. Do you understand?"

"Yes, yes, I understand!" Roland breathed, shimmying closer for his next attempt. His lips and his hands and his heart were nearly bursting with expectation. Tentatively, he reached for her—

"Roland?"

What is it now?

"Hold me tight, sir, you won't break me."

As he kissed her, it seemed to Roland that not even the call of Lucifer himself could have forced him to let that fair maiden go.

He would follow her advice a thousand times with other ladies in the future, and sometimes he would feel something, but never for long, and never, never like this.

THREE

COUNCIL WITH DARKNESS

Roland came awake feeling queasy and lost.

The sweet memory of loving Rosaline was slipping away. He touched his throbbing head and realized that he was lying on the ground.

Slowly, he rolled to his feet. He ached something ugly, but nothing that wouldn't repair itself given time.

He glanced back up at the balcony. He'd never have fallen from it in the old days. Probably shouldn't have worn full armor. He was getting rusty. How many times had he climbed this very wall in anticipation of meeting her? How many times had Rosaline's long blond hair beckoned him like Rapunzel's locks?

Usually, when Roland reached the balcony, she would be waiting, purely elated to see him. She would cry out his name in a hushed whisper, then bound into his arms. She would feel so light, so delicate against him, her skin scented with rose water from her bath, her body almost humming with the power of their secret love—

Roland shook his head. No, their courtship had not been all joy pure and bright. One dark memory tainted the rest.

It was the last memory he had of her.

It came in the third season of their secret courtship, as the world around them turned toward fall and the greens of summer burned away in a riot of flaming oranges and reds..

Together they planned to run away, to escape her father's rule, as well as the prejudices of a society that wouldn't allow a nobleman's daughter to be married to a Moor. Roland had gone away from his love for one week, under the guise of making plans for their new life.

But it had been a lie. He'd gone to seek counsel on the real problems that lay before them:

Would she still love him if she knew?

And:

Could he keep his nature secret from her and still give her a happy life?

Really, there had only been one person to turn to.

He found Cam at the southern tip of the islands that would one day be called New Zealand. Back then, both islands were completely untouched by man. The Maori wouldn't reach the land for another half a century, so Cam had the whole place to himself.

As Roland flew, the cliffs threatened, as sharp as daggers, unlike any he had seen before. The winds bore treacherously down on his wings, tossing him among the clouds. He was shivering and soaked by the time he reached the vast, pristine sound where Cam was hiding from the universe.

The water was a mirror for the mountains, which were green with beech woods. Dipping a wing tip in the water as he passed over its surface, Roland found it icy cold. He shivered and kept on.

At the far end of the sound, he landed on a slate-gray boulder that faced an unfathomably tall waterfall, whose heights were hidden in mists. At its base lay Roland's fallen angel brother, letting his wings be pummeled by the falling water.

What was Cam doing? And how long had he been lying there, in this water-torture chamber of his own making?

"Cam!"

Roland shouted his name three times before he gave up and waded in to pull his brother out. Feeling someone else's touch, Cam flailed and clung to the rocks where he'd lain. But then he recognized Roland and let himself be dragged out, suspicion sharp on his face.

Roland hauled them both onto a rocky ledge behind the falls. It was hard work, and it left him panting, soaking wet, and frozen to his core. The ledge was shallow, but there was enough room for both of them to stand on the damp stone. It was eerily quiet there just behind the roar of the water.

Exhausted, Roland staggered backward until his wings met rock, then slid down and sat.

"Go home, Roland."

Cam's green eyes looked dazed and disoriented as he propped himself up on one elbow. His naked body was one sickly purple bruise from the waterfall's ceaseless beating. But worst of all, his wings—

They were shot through with new gold fibers. Roland couldn't help admiring how brilliantly they shimmered under the moonlight.

"So it's true." Roland had heard the rumors that Cam had crossed over to Lucifer's side.

Neither demon seemed capable of mustering the ritual reserved for greeting new members of the fold. They were meant to embrace, thread their wing tips together as an expression of each one's acceptance of the other, the acknowledgment that they were safe and among friends.

Cam stood, walked over, and spat in Roland's face. "You lack the strength to haul me back into service. Have Lucifer come here himself if he feels I've been neglectful."

Roland wiped his face and pulled himself to his feet. He reached for Cam, but the demon flinched away.

"Cam, I didn't come here to—"

"*I* came here to be alone." Cam moved to a dim corner of the ledge, where Roland could now see a small pile of garments and bags—Cam's few possessions. Roland thought he recognized the parchment scroll that could have been his marriage agreement, but Cam quickly flung a shaggy sheepskin cloak around his body and tucked the parchment into a deep pocket inside. "Oh, you're still here?"

"I need advice, Cam."

"On what? Living the good life?" Cam's spark had come back, but it seemed garish in this pale, shadowy specter standing before Roland. "Start by finding yourself a deserted island. This one's taken, but there must be more out there somewhere." He flung his hand out at the world, at Roland.

"I love a mortal woman," Roland said very slowly. "I want to shape my life around her."

"You don't *have* a life. You're a fallen angel on the other side. You're a *demon*."

"You know what I mean."

"Take it from me. Love is impossible. Get out and save yourself the heartache."

In that moment, Roland realized he'd been foolish to go to Cam for advice. And yet he'd *had* to come. Cam's love story hadn't worked out—but he still understood what Roland was going through.

"Perhaps you could tell me what . . . *not* to do?"

"All right," Cam said, taking a deep, shuddering breath. "Fine. Do *not* demean yourself by living a lie. Do *not* ask me if she will love you if she finds out what you are—even the most lovesick fool knows the answer to that. She will not. She cannot. Do *not* dream that you can keep such a secret from her, either. And above all, for Lucifer's sake, do *not* forget that no temple on earth will have you should you choose to wed this poor creature."

"I believe I can make this work, Cam."

"You believe you and your love see eye to eye, then?"

"Yes. We are devoted to one another."

"And what is her view on eternity?"

Roland paused.

"Don't tell me you don't know? Fine then, I'll tell you. Here, Roland, is the unquestionable truth about our immortality: Mortals cannot fathom it. It frightens them. The knowledge will devour her—that she will grow old and die and you will remain the young and strapping devil that you are."

"I could change for her—I could make myself grow old, appear to wrinkle and wither and—"

"Roland." Cam's face soured. "That isn't your style. Whoever she is, it will be easier on her now, when she is no doubt young and shapely and can find another mate. Don't waste her best years."

"But somehow, love must be possible. Just because you and Lilith couldn't—"

"We're not talking about me."

They stood silently and listened to the echoing of the falling water around them.

"Fine," Roland said at last, "then what about Daniel and Lu—"

"What about them?" Cam roared into the waterfall. His face turned red with sudden fury. "If they're your models, go ask them for advice." He shook his head, disgusted. "We all know what will become of them anyway."

"What do you mean?"

Now Cam turned clear green eyes on Roland. And Roland flushed to find himself being pitied.

"In the end," Cam said, "he will abandon her. He has no choice. He is no match for this curse. It will outlast him and undo him."

Roland's wings bristled. "You're wrong. You have grown too close to Lucifer—"

"That couldn't be further from the truth," Cam

hooted, but when he spun around, Roland noticed the branding on the back of his neck. The tattoo reached just beyond the high collar of his cloak. Unmistakable.

"You wear his mark now?" Roland's voice trembled. He didn't have one. Would never hope to be offered one. Lucifer only branded certain demons, demons with whom he wanted a special relationship.

"Cam, you can't—"

Cam caught Roland's face in his hand and held tight. They stood close, locked in an intimate grip. Roland didn't know if they were enemies or friends.

"Who came to whom to ask for advice, Roland? We are not talking about me and the way I conduct myself. We are talking about you and the pitiful love story that you are going to have to end."

"There must be a way to—"

"Face it: You wouldn't have come to me if you didn't already know the answer."

⁂

Of all the things that Cam had told him that day at the waterfall, his parting words were the hardest ones: Yes, Roland had already known the answer he sought. He'd just hoped that someone would tell him otherwise and save him from having to do what had to be done.

When he came back to tell her, Rosaline seemed already to know. He climbed to her balcony, but she did not rush to kiss him. Her face stiffened in suspicion as soon as he came into her chambers.

"I sense a change in you." Her voice was cold with fear. "What is it?"

Roland's body ached when he saw her look so sad. He did not want to lie to her, but he could not find the words.

"Oh, Rosaline, there is so much I could tell you—"

Then, as if Rosaline remembered his loquacious poems, she demanded: "Answer me in one word. What does our future hold?"

That had been more than a thousand years ago. And still, Roland cringed now, thinking back on what he'd told her. He wished he could smash this memory and the moment with it. But it had happened. And you couldn't change the past.

He had given Rosaline her one word:

"Farewell."

He'd wanted to say, "Forever."

But Cam had spoken truly: Forever wasn't possible between a woman and a fallen angel.

He'd fled before she could beg him not to go. He thought he was being valiant. But life had taught him that he wasn't. He was devastated and scared.

After that, Roland had only seen her once more: two weeks later, when he'd hovered out of sight of her castle window and watched his love weep for one full hour.

After that, he vowed never to cause anyone pain in love. He disappeared.

It became his way.

Roland brushed something from his cheek and was stunned to find it was a tear. Though he'd wiped a million briny drops from other cheeks, he could not recall a time when he himself had cried.

He thought of Lucinda and Daniel, of their eternal devotion to each other. They did not walk away from their mistakes—and over the centuries, they had made many of them. They returned to those mistakes, revisited them, worked through them, until something had at last clicked in this final life, when she was reincarnated as Lucinda Price. It was what had driven her to flee into her past—to find the solution to the curse. So that she and Daniel could be together.

They would always be together. Always have each other, no matter what.

Roland had no one.

Silently, he rose to his feet and made his own Valentine's pledge. He would scale the wall to Rosaline again—and redeem himself the only way he knew how.

FOUR

LOVE'S PUPIL

Back up the outer wall, a second slink along the stone parapet, and then the final sheer ascent to the turret and its balcony and Rosaline once more.

By the time Roland again reached the balcony, the sun was low in the sky, casting long shadows over his shoulder. Announcers shifted and coiled within the shadows, a way of whispering *We are here,* but they left Roland alone. The temperature had dropped, and now the air carried hints of smoke and a coming frost.

He imagined entering the turret via the balcony, stealing through the twilight-dark halls until he found her in her room. And then he pictured her expression:

Images of her staggering backward in amazement, joy plain on her face, hands clenched to her exquisite breast . . .

But what if she was angry?

Still angry, five years later. It was possible.

He shouldn't rule it out.

They'd shared something rare and beautiful, and he'd learned that women felt deeply when it came to love. They felt love in ways Roland could never understand, as if their hearts had extra chambers, vast infinites where love could stay and never leave.

What was he doing here? The wind wove its way beneath his steel armor. He shouldn't be here. This part of his life was over. Cam might have been wrong about love, but he wasn't wrong about how time had changed Roland.

He should climb back down, get on his horse, and find Daniel.

Only . . . he couldn't.

What *could* he do?

He could grovel.

He could drop to his knees and bow before her, beg for forgiveness. He could and he would—

Until this moment, he had not even realized he wanted her forgiveness.

He was near the balcony now, trembling. Was he nervous or excited? He'd come this far, and still he didn't know what he would say. A few lines of a poem formed in the habit's corner of his heart . . .

Let no face reside in mind
But the face of Rosaline.

No—this was where he'd gotten into trouble with her before: She didn't need bad poetry. She needed bodily, reciprocal love.

Could Roland give that to her now?

The red curtain rustled in the wind, then parted at the bold touch of his fingers. He concealed himself behind the stone wall but craned his neck until his gaze entered the bedroom where he used to sit with her.

Rosaline.

She was glorious, sitting in a wooden chair in the corner, singing under her breath. Her face was older, but the years had been kind: She had grown from Roland's girl into a beautiful young woman.

She was glowing.

She was spectacular.

Yes, Roland knew he had made a mistake. He'd been green at love and foolish, cynical and unsure that what they had could last. Too quick to heed Cam's bitter pronouncements.

But look at Luce and Daniel. They had shown

Roland that love could survive even the harshest of punishments. And maybe everything up until this moment—accidentally coming back to this era, agreeing to help Shelby and Miles, riding past Rosaline's old castle—had happened for a reason.

He was being given a second chance at love.

This time, he'd follow his heart. He was ready to bound in through the open window. . . .

But wait—

Rosaline was not singing to herself. Roland blinked, looking again. She had an audience: a small child, swaddled in a feather quilt. The child was nursing. Rosaline was a *mother*.

Rosaline was some man's wife.

Roland's body stiffened and a small gasp escaped his lips. He should have been relieved to see her looking so well—the happiest she'd ever looked—but all he felt was powerfully lonely.

He rolled heavily away from the balcony door, slamming his back against the tower's curved wall. What kind of man had taken the place Roland never should have left?

He dared another look inside, watched as Rosaline got up from the chair and laid the baby in its wooden cradle. Roland closed his eyes and listened to her footsteps fading like a song as she padded out of the room and down the hallway.

This couldn't be the way it ended, his last sight of love.

Fool. Fool to come back. Fool not to leave well enough alone.

Instinctively, he followed her, crawling along the turret's shallow ledge to the next window. He gripped the wall with his abraded fingers.

This chamber, next to the room where he'd seen Rosaline, used to belong to her brother, Geoffrey. But when Roland leaned in to peek through the curved pane, there were women's clothes hanging by the window.

He heard a man's low voice, and then—in reply—Rosaline's.

A young man sat with his back to Roland at the edge of a damask-covered bed. When he turned his head, his profile was handsome, but not devastatingly so. Smooth brown hair, freckled skin, an honest sloping nose.

A woman lay sprawled across him on the bed, her blond head nestled in his lap in the casual way of two people who were as comfortable with each other's limbs as they were with their own. She was weeping.

She was Rosaline.

"But why, Alexander?"

When she raised her tear-streaked face to look at him, Roland's heart caught in his throat.

Alexander—her husband—stroked his wife's tangled blond hair. "My love." He kissed her nose, the last place

Roland would have gone had he had access to those lips. "My horse is saddled. The men await me at the barracks. You know that I must leave before nightfall to join them."

Rosaline gripped the white sleeve of his undershirt and sobbed. "My father has a thousand knights who can take your place. I pray you, do not leave me—do not leave *us*—to go and fight."

"Your father has already been too generous. Why should another man take my place when I am young and able? It is my duty, Rosaline. I must go. When our crusade is done, I will return to you."

She shook her head, her cheeks pink with fury. "I cannot bear to lose you. I cannot live without you."

Roland's heart stuttered at the words.

"You won't have to," Alexander said. "I give you my word: I shall return."

He rose from the bed, helping his wife to her feet. Roland noticed with renewed jealousy that she was pregnant with another child. Her belly protruded under the fine ruched gown. She rested her hands on it, despondent.

Roland would never be able to leave her in a state like that. How could this man go off to war? What war mattered in the face of love's obligations?

Any heartache she might have felt for Roland five years ago paled in comparison to this, because this man was not only her lover and her husband—he was also the father of her children.

Roland's heart sagged. He could not abide this. He thought of all those years between this medieval heartbreak and the present he'd come back from—the centuries he'd spent on the moon, wandering lost through its crags and pocks, abandoning his duties, just trying to forget he had ever seen her. He thought of the void of time he'd surrendered inside the portal that connected July to September, abandoning everything the way he had abandoned Rosaline.

But now he knew that no matter how long his infinity lasted, he would never forget her tears.

What a narcissistic fool he had been. She didn't need his apology—to apologize to her now would be wholly selfish, just Roland seeking relief for his guilty conscience. And opening her wounds anew. There was nothing he could do or be for Rosaline anymore.

Or almost nothing.

※

The young man looked lanky and uncoordinated as he approached the stable where Roland waited. He carried his helmet in his hand, leaving his face exposed. Roland studied it. He hated and respected this man, who clearly felt both obligated and reluctant to fight. Could honor and duty mean more to him than love? Or maybe this confusion of honor and duty *was* love—paradoxes piled higher than the furthest reaches of the stars.

Who would want to go to war and leave a loving family?

"Soldier," Roland called to Alexander when he was close enough to recognize the torment in his eyes. "You are Alexander, kin of my lord John, who holds the title of this fief?"

"And who are you?" Alexander stepped across the threshold of the stable. His pale brown eyes narrowed as they took in Roland's formal armor. "What battle have you come from, dressed like that?"

"I have been sent here to take your place in the campaign."

Alexander stopped. "My wife sent you? Her father?" He shook his head. "Step aside, soldier. Let me ride on."

"Indeed, I will not. Your assignment has changed. You know the terrain in this vicinity better than most. Dangerous times may be upon us if the battle does not favor us in the North. If we retreat, you will be needed here to guard the city from intruders."

Alexander tilted his head. "Show your face, soldier, for I do not trust a man who hides behind a mask."

"My face is no concern of yours."

"Who are you?"

"A man who knows that your duty is here among

your family. All the spoils of war matter not in the face of true love and familial honor. Now, stand down if you wish to live."

Alexander let out a soft laugh, but then his expression changed into something harder. He drew his sword. "Let's have it, then."

Roland should have expected this. And yet it galled him. How could this man be so intent on leaving her? Roland would never leave her!

And yet, of course, he already had. Abandoned his one true love like a callous, stupid fool. He had been alone ever since. Solitude was one thing, but it warped into ugly, wretched loneliness after the soul had tasted love.

No man should be allowed to make the same mistake. Even through his jealousy, Roland could see that. It fell to him to stop Alexander.

He swallowed, sighed inwardly, and drew his sword. It was a meter long and as sharp as the pain stabbing his heart at having to confront this man. "Soldier," Roland said flatly. "I do not jest."

The man advanced, waving his sword awkwardly. Roland deflected it with an effortless flick of the wrist. The blades clashed dully.

Alexander's slid earthward with the lightest guidance from Roland's blade, until it glanced off the wet hay on the floor of the stable.

"Why would you so willingly ride to your own death?" Roland asked.

Alexander grunted and lurched back into fighting position, raising his blade chest high. "I am not a coward."

Perhaps not, but he was exceptionally unskilled. He had probably picked up some swordsmanship as a child, jousting at haystacks at summer festivals with his boyhood friends. He was no soldier. He'd be dead in an hour on the front.

Or Roland could kill him now. . . .

In that moment, he had a vision of his blade swinging deftly down on this man's bare neck. The shock of a severed spine and the slick red blood dripping from the steel onto the dirt.

How easy to end this man's short life. Take his place up in that tower and love her as she needed to be loved. Roland knew how to do it now.

But then he blinked and saw Rosaline. The baby.

Do not slaughter, he reminded himself. *Only persuade.*

He leaped forward lightly, swinging his sword toward Alexander, who scrambled backward, spinning wildly away. This time he avoided Roland's blade by sheer luck.

Roland laughed and his laughter tasted bitter. "I am offering you a boon, soldier—and I promise you, I follow a higher command than your liege. Know that I will not dishonor your intentions. Let me go to war for you."

"You speak in riddles." Alexander's fear had stretched the skin around his mouth tight as a leather drum. "You cannot replace me."

"Yes," Roland said, seething. "If nothing else, at least I know *that*."

In a burst of violence, Roland forgot his purpose. He went at Alexander with the fury of a lover scorned. In the face of Roland's blade, Alexander stood rigid, sword extended. To his credit, he did not back away. But with another clash of their swords, Roland had disarmed Alexander. He held his blade's tip at the young man's heaving throat.

"A true knight would yield. He would accept my offer and serve his people here, protecting his home and his neighbors when they need protection." Roland swallowed. "Do you yield, sir?"

Alexander gasped for air, unable to speak. He kept casting his eyes downward to the blade at his neck. He was terrified. He nodded. He would yield.

A calm came over Roland, and he let himself close his eyes.

He and this pale mortal Alexander loved the same bright thing. They could not be enemies. It was then that Roland chose his side. He would not spare Alexander's life for Alexander's sake, but for Rosaline's.

"You are a braver man than I." And it was true, for Alexander had been strong enough to love Rosaline when Roland was too afraid. "Embrace the luck I give you this night and return to your family." He had to work to keep his voice steady. "Kiss your wife and raise your children. *That* is honor."

They held each other's gaze for a long, tense moment, until Roland began to feel that Alexander could see through the slit in his visor. How could Alexander not feel the ache in the air between them? How could he not sense how close Roland had come to killing him and taking his place?

Roland withdrew his sword from Alexander's neck. He sheathed his weapon, mounted his horse, and rode out of the stable into the night.

⇥⇤

The road was bare and blue in the moonlight.

Roland headed north. He still needed to find Daniel—at least one love should be redeemed in this joust with time. For a quarter of an hour, Roland lost himself in thoughts of Rosaline, but the memory was too painful to indulge for long. His eyes refocused on the road when he saw a rider galloping toward him on a coal-black horse.

Even in the darkness, there was something strange and yet familiar about the knight's armor. For a moment, Roland wondered whether it was his own former self, but when the knight put up a hand to slow Roland's ride, his gestures were more urgent than Roland's would have been.

They stopped before one another, their horses whickering as they circled, breathing frost.

"You come from yonder estate?" The knight's voice boomed across the road as he pointed toward the castle in the distance.

He must have thought Roland was Alexander. Had this knight been sent to escort Alexander to the front?

"Y-yes," Roland stammered. "I am a replacement for—"

"Roland?" The soldier's voice changed from what Roland realized was a hoarse, affected boom into something effervescent and fantastically charming.

The knight threw off his helmet. Black hair rolled like rapids down the suit of armor, and then, in the moonlight, Roland saw the face he'd known better than any other since the dawn of time.

"Arriane!"

They leaped from their horses and into each other's arms. Roland didn't know how long it had been since his medieval self had seen this medieval Arriane, but the emotional battle he'd just survived made it feel like centuries had passed since he'd last seen a friend.

He spun the wiry angel around. Her wings bloomed

out of slits in her armor, and Roland envied her their freedom. Of course her clothes would be tailored for wings—all of them had been back then.

Roland felt caged in his borrowed metal suit, but he didn't want to complain to Arriane. She did not know yet that he was an Anachronism, and he wanted to keep it that way. He was so glad to see her.

The moonlight shone like a spotlight on his friend's white skin. When she turned her head, Roland gasped.

A horrific burn glistened on the left side of her neck. The skin was marbled, knotted, bleeding, the most gruesome kind of wound. Roland recoiled without meaning to, making Arriane self-conscious.

She reached up to cover the wound but groaned when her fingers grazed it.

Roland had seen this scar a thousand times in future encounters with Arriane, but its origin remained a mystery to him. Only one thing could hurt an angel that way, but he'd never known how to ask her about it.

The wound was fresh now, like a rash of flames across her neck. She must have sustained the injury only recently.

"Arriane, what happened to you?"

She looked away, not meaning to give Roland an even clearer view of her ravaged skin. She sniffed. "Love is hell."

"But"—Roland closed his eyes, hearing the line repeating itself in his mind—"an angel's form cannot be marred, except by . . ." Arriane looked away in shame, and Roland drew her to him. "Oh, Arriane!" he cried, clasping his arms around her waist, his eyes drawn to and repelled by her neck. He could not embrace her as he wanted to, could not squeeze away the pain. "I ache for you."

She nodded. She knew. She had never liked to cry. She said, "I've just come from seeing Daniel."

"I was on my way to meet him," Roland said, breathless with the luck of it. "His presence is required at Saint Valentine's Faire."

"He rides to town this evening. He may well be there already. Lucinda will be happy, at least."

"Yes," Roland said, remembering more clearly now. "*You* were the knight who came to deliver that message to the others in the camp. It wasn't me. You forged the king's decree that told the men to take their Valentine's leave."

Arriane crossed her arms over her chest. "How did you know that?"

"Clairvoyant." He was surprised to find himself smiling.

It was enough to have her here, his dearest friend. It made this journey into his past heartbreak a little less bleak.

Roland picked up Arriane's helmet, helped her back

onto her horse. He mounted and dropped his visor once again. Side by side, the two knights rode for the city.

Sometimes love was not about winning, but about wise sacrifice and the reliability of friends like Arriane. Friendship, Roland realized, was its very own kind of love.

BURNING LOVE

THE VALENTINE OF ARRIANE

ONE

THE SECRET

Arriane looked out at the thyme-scented Tuscan morning and sighed.

She was sprawled on green-velvet grass, propped on her elbows with her chin in her palms, relishing the unseasonable warmth and the sensation of soft fingers running through her long dark hair.

This was how Arriane and Tess spent their rare afternoons together: One girl braided, the other spun stories. Then they switched roles.

"Once there was an extraordinary angel," Arriane began, turning her head to the side so Tess could sweep the hair up from her neck.

Tess was better at braiding than Arriane. She would sit beside Arriane with a basket of forest wildflowers in her lap. She'd lean over Arriane's narrow back and weave tight plaits into the angel's thick hair. She'd pin the braids so they zigzagged across Arriane's scalp, until she looked like Medusa, which was Arriane's favorite style.

Arriane, on the other hand, was lucky to get Tess's wild red mop into a single crooked braid. She'd pull and tug and wrestle the comb through Tess's locks until Tess yelped in pain. But Arriane was better at storytelling. And what would braiding be without a good story?

No fun at all.

Arriane closed her eyes and moaned as Tess's fingernails swiveled up her scalp. Nothing felt so good as a lover's touch.

"Arriane?"

"Yes." Her eyes opened, her gaze drifting over the pasture where dairy cows loafed on the farm's two hundred acres. These were her favorite moments: quiet and uncomplicated, just the two of them. It was late in the afternoon; most of the milkmaids who worked on the farm where Arriane had taken her employment were already back at their cottages.

She'd chosen this job because it wasn't far from Lucinda, who, in this lifetime, had grown up in an English fiefdom a few minutes' fly north. Generally, Daniel felt stifled by the presence of Arriane and the other angels tasked with watching over him. But from the dairy, Arriane could give him space and still fly to him and Lucinda quickly if needed. Besides, Arriane enjoyed dipping into a mortal lifestyle every once in a while. It felt good to be given work on the dairy, to satisfy a boss. Tess never understood that urge, but then, Tess's master was a little more demanding than the Throne.

It was rare to have a stolen moment with Tess. Her visits to the dairy—to this part of the world, in general—never came quickly or lasted long enough. Arriane didn't like to imagine the darkness that awaited Tess as soon as they said goodbye, or the master who hated to see Tess straying from his realm.

Don't think about him, Arriane chided herself. *Not when Tess is by your side and there is no need to question your love!*

Yes. Tess was by her side. And the grass beneath was so soft, the air of the farm so perfumed with wildflowers, that Arriane could have wafted into the nurturing bosom of a reassuring dream.

But the story. Tess loved her stories. "Where was I?" Arriane asked.

"Oh—I don't remember." Tess sounded distracted.

Her fingernail scraped Arriane's neck as she scooped up a section of hair.

"Ouch." Arriane rubbed her neck. Tess didn't *remember*? But Arriane was the one who got lost in her thoughts, not Tess. "Is something wrong, love?"

"No," Tess said quickly. "You were starting some story. . . . An extraordinary . . . um—"

"Yes!" Arriane said happily. "An *extraordinary* angel. Her name was . . . Arriane."

Tess tugged her hair. "Another one about you?" She was laughing, but her laughter sounded distant, as if she had already flown far away.

"You're in it, too! Just wait." Arriane rolled onto her side to face Tess. The arm Tess had been braiding with slid down across Arriane's hip.

Tess wore a white cotton gown with a narrow bodice and short, ruffled white sleeves. She had bursts of freckles on her shoulders, which Arriane thought looked like galaxies of stars. Her eyes were barely darker than Arriane's startling pale blue irises.

She was the most beautiful creature Arriane had ever met.

"And what was so extraordinary about this angel?" Tess asked after a moment, picking up her cue.

"Oh, where to begin? There were *so* many extraordinary things about her!" Arriane flicked her head, musing on an inspired direction in which to take her tale. She could feel the unbound braid scissoring loose on the side of her head.

"Oh, Arriane!" Tess said. "You've ruined it!"

"I can't help it if my hair has other plans! And maybe yours does, too!" Arriane reached for the ribbon tied around Tess's long red braid.

But the girl was too quick. She scrambled backward in the grass like a crab, laughing as Arriane rose to her feet and chased after her.

"This *most* extraordinary angel," she called after Tess, who dashed through the high grass and the bracing February wind, "had the most *disgusting* nest of tangles in her hair. She was famous for it, far and wide. Tanglelocks, some called her." Arriane high-stepped, her hands raised, her fingers wiggling to evoke her hair. "Cities vanished in her mighty mane. Whole armies were swept up in her snarls! Grown men wept and were lost in the black abyss of her serpentine tresses."

Then Arriane tripped over the long hem of her shapeless milkmaid's gown and went down hard onto the ground. On all fours, she looked up at Tess, who'd stopped between Arriane and the sun, a halo of light circling her red hair.

Tess leaned down to help Arriane up, her hands soft around Arriane's wrists.

"Until one day"—Arriane went to rub her muddy palms on the front of her dress; Tess slapped them away and produced, from her stringed pocket, a cotton hand-kerchief. "One day, this angel met someone who changed her life. . . ."

Tess lifted her chin a bit. She was listening.

"This person was a little devil," Arriane said. "She was rather serious, always thwarting Tangelocks's pranks, always mocking her ingenuity, always reminding Tangelocks that some things were more important than plain old *hair*."

Unexpectedly, Tess turned away. She sat down in the grass with her back to Arriane. Perhaps she'd found her character's introduction unflattering? But there was more to come! Every story required a turning point, an element of surprise. Arriane sprawled across Tess's stretched-out legs and propped herself up on one elbow in the grass. With her other hand, she reached to un-cross the arms Tess had fixed firmly over her chest. But even with her hands clasped in her lover's, Tess's eyes would not be wrested from the pale yellow wildflower in the grass.

"Abandon this silly story, Arriane." She spoke as if in a trance. "I am not in the mood for it today."

"Oh, but wait! I'm just getting warmed up!" Arriane furrowed her brow. "In so many ways this seeming adversary was the dire opposite of Tangelocks. Her hair was a red dandelion pouf." Arriane stroked Tess's hair. "Her skin was a pale canvas that burned at the slightest touch of the sun." She ran her finger down Tess's smooth, bare arm.

"Arriane—"

"But the creature was a demon with a comb, and in her hands were tamed the destructive locks. This person's nature, unlike the angel's, was—"

"Enough!" Tess snapped, jerking her gaze away and toward a shallow, pebble-lined stream at the edge of the pasture. "I'm tired of fairy tales."

She stood up and Arriane scrambled to join her.

"It's not a fairy tale," Arriane insisted, ignoring the goose bumps she felt rising on her skin. She sat up straight and tilted her head at Tess. "The fact that we're here together—"

"Is only a sign that he wasn't paying attention."

"Wasn't?" A cold wind crept over the meadow.

"He has given me an ultimatum."

The blood drained from Arriane's cheeks, and with it went the brilliant colors in the meadow. The blue sky dimmed, the grass lost its verve. Even Tess's hair seemed pale. Arriane had known this moment was coming—had known it ever since the start—but still it took her breath away.

Tess bore the black starburst tattoo on the back of her neck, the one Lucifer branded on his innermost circle of demons.

"He knows. And now he wants me back." There was

ice in Tess's voice, ice that seemed to creep across Arriane's soul.

"But you just got here!" Arriane felt like running to her love, falling at Tess's feet and weeping, but she just stared down at her hands. "I don't want you to leave. I hate it when you go away."

"Arriane—" Tess took a step toward her, but Arriane flinched, enraged.

"It's not his business to say what we can and can't do! What kind of monster boasts so incessantly about free will and yet won't let you be free to follow your own heart?"

"I don't have a choice about this."

"Yes, you do," Arriane said. "You just won't make it."

When Tess didn't answer, Arriane's chest heaved with the initial wave of a tsunami-sized sob. She felt so ashamed. She turned and ran across the pasture. She ran along the streambed and up the soft slope of grass at the western edge of the farm. She trampled through her mistress's herb garden, unable to see the thyme through her tears. She could hear Tess running after her, her soft footsteps catching up. But Arriane did not stop until she'd reached the door of the old barn where tomorrow morning she would rise just before dawn to do the milking.

She threw herself against the rough wood wall of the barn and let the sobs come.

Tess hugged Arriane from behind, her red braid swinging over Arriane's shoulder. She laid her head between Arriane's shoulder blades and they stood like that, both of them crying, for a quiet moment.

When Arriane turned around, leaning her back against the sun-warm wall of the barn, Tess took her hand. Her fingers were long and pale and slender; Arriane's were tiny, the nails chewed to the quick. Arriane drew Tess through the open rusty-hinged door inside the barn, where they would be safe from the eyes of the other milkmaids, who would be gathering for supper soon.

They stood among hay and horses, a few cows lying curled together in a corner. The scents of the animals were everywhere: the horses' musk, the chickens' downy sweetness, the dried sweat of the cows' hides.

"There is a way for us to be together," Tess said to Arriane in a low voice.

"How? You would defy him?"

"No, Arriane." The demon shook her head. "I took my oath. I am bound to Lucifer."

When Tess turned her head to gaze out the barn's door and across the endless meadow, Arriane glimpsed the dark starburst tattoo that marred her lovely skin. It was the sole blemish that could adhere to angels' bodies. Except for their wing scars, every other ink mark or wound or scar in time would fade away.

Lucifer's mark was the only part of Tess that Arriane could say she did not love. She reached up to touch her own neck, pale and unblemished. Pure.

"There is another way," Tess said, pressing close to Arriane so that their feet overlapped. Tess's love smelled like jasmine, and she often said that Arriane smelled of sweet cream. "A way to stop living like this, with everything between us always a secret."

Tess extended her arms toward Arriane and reached around her shoulders. Arriane thought for a moment that they were going to embrace again. She felt her body drawing in, needing to be held—

Instead, cold fingers crawled up the back of her neck. "You could join me."

Arriane lurched away. Her skin crawled.

"Join me as my soul mate, Arriane. Join me and take your place among the ranks of Hell."

TWO

INFERNAL DESIRES

Arriane recoiled. "No," she whispered, certain of its impossibility. "I could never."

Tess's blue eyes pleaded with a fierce intensity. "We can end our secret affair and proclaim it to the universe."

The way her voice boomed, echoing off the rafters in the barn, made Arriane nervous.

"Don't you want that?" Tess cried. "Don't you want to be together, to snap the arbitrary shackles that prevent us from being our true selves?"

Arriane shook her head. This was unfair. Tess was out of her mind. She had the most sublimely beautiful soul Arriane had ever seen, but this time, she had gone too far. If she cared for Arriane at all, Tess would already know what her lover's answer would be.

But then—

Arriane wavered, allowing herself for a moment to see the situation from Tess's point of view. Of course Arriane wanted to love Tess openly. She always would. What else did she have to do to prove it?

No! How could Tess ask this of her? To side with Hell over Heaven! That wasn't love. That was insanity.

"Maybe the rules are right," Arriane said tentatively. "Maybe angels and demons shouldn't—"

"What?" Tess cut her off. "Say it."

"Lucifer would never allow it," Arriane finally said evasively, turning away from Tess to pace the barn. She passed the horses in their stables. The cows in their pen. Everything had its place. She looked across the barn at Tess and had never felt further away from the soul she loved the most.

"Lucifer might allow it—" Tess started to say.

"You know how he feels about love!" Arriane snapped. "Ever since . . ." But she trailed off. That old story didn't matter, not right now.

"You don't understand." Tess laughed a false laugh, as if Arriane were failing to understand something as simple as an arithmetic problem. "He said that if I brought you with me—"

"Who said?" Arriane's head snapped up. *"Lucifer?"*

Tess stepped away, as if afraid, and for a moment, Arriane thought she saw something in the rafters of the barn. A stone statue . . . a gargoyle. He seemed to be watching them. But when she blinked he was gone. She found Tess's wild eyes again, and she felt betrayed.

"You told him?"

Now Arriane marched toward Tess, stopping just short of her lover's breast. It heaved with surprise at being confronted, but Tess did not back away.

"How dare you," Arriane spat, spinning on her heel.

Before Arriane could run out of the barn, Tess grabbed hold of her wrists. Arriane wrenched away, feeling Tess's fingers drag against her skin.

"Leave me be!" Arriane shouted, not meaning it, but Tess wasn't listening anyway. She came at Arriane again, yanking on the sleeve of her gown so hard the fabric ripped.

"Yes, I told him!" Tess bellowed, shouting right into Arriane's face. "Unlike you, I don't care who knows!"

Arriane pushed her. She pushed her so hard, Tess fell backward into a tower of stacked milk pails. They toppled over, falling on her with a clatter, splattering her pale skin with a few white drops.

Tess kicked the pails away and rocketed to her feet.

And then—Arriane had not been expecting this—her wings bloomed out behind her shoulders.

They *never* exposed their wings to each other; it was something they'd agreed on ages ago. It was too plain a reminder that their love was not meant to be.

Now Tess's broad demon wings filled the barn with shimmery light. They were the gold of the last moment of a sunset, tall slopes that rose high behind her shoulders like twin mountain peaks. They beat lightly at her sides, fully extended, rigid, with the tips curled slightly outward in Arriane's direction.

The ritual fighting stance.

The horses whinnied and the cows began to bleat as if they could sense the tension, the brink of something bad.

What happened next, Arriane did not intend—but she also could not help it: Her wings responded to the call. They bloomed out from her shoulders in a rush that felt so innately good, she let out a heedless cry of joy. But in the next moment she choked with regret to see them billowing out at her sides.

Tess beat her great golden wings, and her body rose. She hovered in the air for a fraction of a second before she lunged down, tackling Arriane. The two of them rolled to the floor of the barn.

"Why are you doing this?" Arriane cried, gripping Tess's shoulders, straining to hold her back as they wrestled.

Tess had a fistful of Arriane's long hair. She jerked it backward to look Arriane in the eye. "To show you I would fight for you. I would do anything for you."

"Let me go!" Arriane did not want to fight her love, but her wings felt the old magnetic pull toward the eternal foe. Arriane screamed out in pain and slapped the face she'd only ever wanted to dote on.

"Once you join me," Tess fumed, pinning Arriane's hands to the ground, "he will accept you. He will accept our love."

Arriane shook her head, cowering beneath her lover. She was afraid of what Tess would do next, but she had to tell the truth.

"It's a trick."

"Shut up."

"A trick to get me down there. One more soul is all he wants." Arriane strained against her lover's grasp, against her own leaden wings, which cast sparks each time they brushed against Tess's. "Lucifer is a merchant," she shouted over the din of their brawl, "staying in the market after sundown just to make one last sale. As soon as I joined you—"

Tess froze, her flushed face an inch above Arriane's. She let go of Arriane's hair, unleashed her from where she was pinned to the ground. She cupped a hand to Arriane's cheek. "So you'll consider it?"

There was so much heat in Tess's blue gaze that Arriane's heart melted.

"I can remember the first time I said goodbye to you," Tess whispered. "I was so afraid I'd never see you again."

Arriane shivered. "Oh, Tessriel."

How could she resist one final kiss? The fight dissolved as her head lifted toward Tess, whose whole face changed. Love flooded back in, filling the space between their bodies until there was no space between them. They threaded their fingers through each other's hair, limbs entwined, and held each other close. When their lips met, Arriane's whole body ignited with frustrated passion. She drank her love in, never wanting to break from this embrace, knowing that when it was over . . .

They would be over.

Her eyes drifted open and she gazed upon her true love's peaceful face. Arriane could never really think of Tess as a demon. Never.

She would remember her like this.

Without her realizing it, her lips had pulled away from Tess's. Her heart was heavy, cumbersome, and sad.

She sat up slowly, then rose to her feet. "I—I cannot join you."

Tess's eyes narrowed and her voice grew shockingly cold, the way it did when her pride was wounded. She didn't get up from the ground. "You're a fallen angel, Arriane. It is time you realize it and come down from your altar."

"I am not that kind of fallen angel." *I am not like you.* "I fell because I believe in love."

"That's a lie! You fell because Daniel dragged you and me and everyone else down with him."

Arriane flinched. "At least Daniel's brand of love doesn't require that one person betray her nature."

"Are you so sure of that?"

The question hung in the air. Arriane walked to the trough against the far wall and added feed and a bucket of well water to the horses' bins. She heard Tess sigh.

"I believe in Daniel's cause," Arriane said. "I believe in Lucinda."

"Wrong again, you were *assigned* to them. You *have* to look after them or those idiots from the Scale will come for you."

"It doesn't mean I don't believe! I won't give up on Lucinda and Daniel."

"Instead you would give up on us?" Tess was crying now; she sat in the center of the barn and wiped her tears on her muddy handkerchief. "Tomorrow is Valentine's Day, Arriane."

"I know. We agreed to fly to Saint Valentine's Faire, where Lucinda and Daniel and all the others will be." Arriane's voice wobbled. "We were going to be merry."

"Merry? Pretending I am not your love and you are not mine? Pretending to search for what we already share?" Tess scowled.

Arriane didn't answer. Tess was right. Their predicament was excruciating.

Tess stood at last and drew close to Arriane. She took the pail from her hands and set it on the ground. She cupped a hand to Arriane's cheek. "Let Luce and Daniel have their Valentine's Day. Let us have ours. Celebrate true love by making a covenant with me. Join me, Arriane. We could be so happy together—if we were *truly* together."

Arriane swallowed the fear rising in her throat. "I love you, but I can't turn my back on my promises."

She moved from Tess's grip. Arriane's eyes raced to capture every detail about Tess: the slow sway of her red hair in the breeze, her pale bare feet in the rough straw, her hand making the shape of Arriane's hand's absence, tears rising in her bright blue eyes.

Even the spectacular golden gleam of her wings.

This would be the last time they would see each other. This would be their last goodbye.

TWO

THE FIRST CUT IS
THE DEEPEST

Never.

Never.

Never.

Arriane's soul was heavy as she flew. She should have known this was coming! She *had* known. Something in her soul had long felt that a day like this approached, when Lucifer would call Tessriel back.

But she had *never* expected Tess to ask her to give up her place in Heaven—to trade it for the fires of Hell!

Her temper flared now and her wings flexed and strained in response.

Sometimes when Arriane stayed too long in mortal guise, she forgot how vast her wings were, how strong, how deep the pleasure of letting them out from her shoulders, the winged energy of delight. She should have been feeling the exaltation she always felt when soaring through the sky, but now her silver wings were just sad reminders of what she was, and of what her love was, and of how she and Tess could never be together.

Never.

I can remember the first time I said goodbye to you, Tess had told her in the barn. *I was so afraid I'd never see you again.*

Arriane remembered it, too: thousands of years ago. She and Annabelle and Gabbe had been hovering in a dark rain cloud on the outskirts of a place called Canaan, watching a mortal celebration led by a man named Abraham, when the angel appeared out of nowhere and hovered before them in the sky.

"Who are you?" Gabbe was hostile, addressing the angel with the bright-red hair and crystal-blue eyes. To Arriane, the unknown angel's wings were lovely, and her body looked as soft as a cumulus cloud. Lightning flashed across her radiant white skin. Arriane remembered wanting to reach out and touch her, as if to make certain the angel was real.

"I am Tessriel, your former sister in Heaven." The unfamiliar angel had bowed her head in deference. "Angel of the thunder that rolls across Eurasia."

Tessriel was looking at Arriane, and something in a distant meadow of Arriane's soul recalled this angel. Her sister. Yes. They hadn't known each other well in Heaven—there had been a league of other angels between them, but there had always been a connection. That inexplicable mystery called attraction.

"I bring news of your brother Roland," Tessriel said to Arriane, who had gasped at the sound of his name.

"Roland resides in Lucifer's domain," Gabbe said sharply. "You bring us news from Hell?"

"I bring you news—" Tessriel's voice wavered and Arriane's heart went out to her. She hadn't seen Roland since the Fall and she missed him desperately. This angel had come with a message. Arriane scrambled forward, pressing up against Gabbe, who held her back with the white edge of her wing.

"Go now, leave us be," Gabbe commanded. It was final.

Tessriel shook her head sadly as she turned to go. She looked back once at Arriane, briefly and with great sorrow. "Goodbye."

"Goodbye!"

※

But it wasn't goodbye. Years later, on her own, walking the shoals of a mortal river, she came upon the red-haired angel again.

"Tessriel?"

Tessriel looked up from the river, where she was bathing. She was naked, her pure-white wings skimming the surface of the water, and her long red hair trailing slickly down her back.

"Is it you?" Tessriel whispered. "I thought I'd never see you again."

When the angel rose from the river, the sight of her mortal guise was too much for Arriane, who looked away, thrilled and embarrassed. She heard the ripple of wings leaving water, felt a brush of warm wind, and then, a second later, the sweetest lips pressed down on hers. Wet arms and wet wings engulfed her.

"What was that?" Arriane blinked in astonishment as Tessriel pulled away. Her lips tingled with unexpected desire.

"A kiss. I promised myself that if I did see you again, that's what I would do."

"And if I left right now and then came back," Arriane wondered aloud, "would you kiss me like that again?"

Tessriel nodded, a vast smile on her face.

"Goodbye," Arriane whispered, closing her eyes. When she opened them, she said, "Hello."

And Tessriel kissed her again.

And again.

On a dark fjord north of Norway . . . on a ship setting sail for the Indies . . . on a dusty desert plateau in Persia . . . or in a rainstorm inside a rain forest—when the world was uncomplicated and young and neither fallen angel had yet turned in the direction each would ultimately turn in, Arriane and Tessriel were always saying goodbye to say hello again, always moving in or out of a kiss.

⊰⊱

Now, feeling as far as she ever had from the lips of the demon she'd loved, Arriane passed a pair of herons in the sky. They were paired, but she had to be alone. Because of old allegiances neither would betray. It drove her mad with frustration. She needed to be someplace lonesome and remote, where her heart could ache in peace.

Tears blurred her vision as she climbed over the low-lying meadows of the valley below. She didn't want to leave Tess; she couldn't leave quickly enough. Soon, she had escaped the dairy in its little verdant vale, which she had grown to love.

Love. What was it, anyway?

Daniel and Lucinda seemed to know. There had been moments when Arriane thought she danced toward love's awareness: tender, fleeting moments locked in a kiss with Tess, when both souls lost themselves completely. If only they could have stayed like that forever, lying to themselves in an extended state of bliss.

Maybe love was lying to yourself.

No. The world bore down on them, and in the broad, clear light of day, Arriane knew that what she felt for Tess both was and was not love. It was everything—and it was impossible.

It was why they had already been through this kind of goodbye, the ugly kind, once before.

It was a few hundred years after the Fall. Arriane had finally made her choice. She had been back to the plains of Heaven and, after some time, had made her peace with the Throne. Her wings shone a terrific iridescent silver—the mark that she was accepted once again—and Arriane was eager to show them off to her love. She found Tessriel under the Amazonian waterfall where they had agreed to meet.

"Look what I've done—"

"What have you done?"

Just as Arriane's wings bore a brand-new silver shine, Tessriel's wings were tainted—a glorious, gaudy gold.

"You never told me you were considering . . ." Arriane's voice trailed off.

"You never told me, either." Tess's eyes welled up with tears, but as soon as she wiped them away, she looked angry.

"But why? Why would you side with him?"

"Isn't your choice as arbitrary as mine? Your master is only the authority because you say he is."

"At least he is *good*, unlike your master!"

"*Good. Evil.* They're just words, Arriane. Who can trust them, anyway?"

"How—how can I love you now?" Arriane whispered.

"It's simple," Tess said with a sad shake of her head. "You can't."

⚜

It was Roland who brought them back together. Now Arriane almost wished he hadn't. But at the time, she had needed Tess more than she ever would have admitted. Roland arranged for a stolen moment between the two in Jerusalem, after what was supposed to be Cam's marriage to Lilith.

That marriage hadn't happened.

But Arriane and Tessriel had. As soon as they saw each other, their argument dissolved into another unstoppable kiss.

"We must be free to each be ourselves independently," Tessriel had told her, "but we shall never be as strong and solid as we are when we're together."

"Be careful," Roland was always saying when she would sneak off to be with Tess. And Arriane was. Never once did they get caught. Never once did the angels suspect Arriane's secret romance with one of Lucifer's closest demons. She had been careful about so much—except the destiny of her heart.

She simply had never expected Tessriel to make her choose.

But now it had come to that, and there was only one choice.

This goodbye had to be forever.

⚜

Arriane couldn't breathe. Tears streamed down her cheeks now as she gasped and blindly flew on, not knowing where she'd go.

Would she ever see her love again?

A sharp pain seemed to pierce her heart, an agony riddled its way into the fissures of her bones. What was happening? Then a dark premonition sapped at her soul, and Arriane cried out in fear.

She clutched her heart, but this wasn't mere heartache.

Something was wrong.

Tess.

In the middle of her flight across the mountains of northern Italy, Arriane swooped around to reverse directions in the sky. Her wings shuddered and her heart stalled and the only thing she knew was that she had to get back to the dairy farm. It was a lover's intuition, a slow consciousness spreading through her brain. . . .

Until she was absolutely certain . . .

Something had happened—

Something unspeakable.

THREE

LOVE TAKES WING

The barn was empty.

The sun had set.

The only light besides a cold sliver of Tuscan moon shining through the open door came from Arriane's wings. They cast a soft, opalescent glow on the animals, which were not sleeping: The horses whinnied and the chickens clucked restlessly in their pens; the cows lay in the musky hay, their udders swollen with milk.

They sensed something, too.

Arriane grew frantic—where was Tess? She paced the barn, searching for clues, finding only the evidence of their fight. The toppled milk pails. The scuffed patch of muddy hay where they had tussled. If she closed her eyes, she could still see Tess the way she wanted to, smiling, the bright flush in her cheeks.

Arriane's breath made clouds before her face. She watched them vanish into the frosty air. She wanted to scream, to stop every disappearing thing.

The premonition was so strong that Arriane wrung her hands, retracing her steps around the stables before she'd stormed off into the sky, remembering the angry words they had spat at each other, regretting everything she'd ever said or done to Tess that did not come from a place of utter love.

There.

She froze as her wing tip dragged across a mound of damp hay.

What was that?

Arriane dropped to her knees. Her wings glowed white, illuminating the terrified animals, which were backed into the corners of their stalls.

There was blood on the hay—a shiny, red pool.

"Tessriel!"

Arriane soared upward, scanning the ground madly for another trace of her love's blood. She flew in a panicked circle, scouring every inch of the barn, darting like a skylark this way and that, finding nothing.

Until she let her wings carry her outside, to the far side of the barn.

There, just beyond the open doorway, she spied a small well of blood seeping into the grass. She moved closer, hovering over it. She wanted to touch it, but—

No. She stopped herself.

Stretching away from the pool of blood, dark-red beaded drops formed a string several inches long, leading in the direction of the North Star.

Tess was on the move. But what had happened to her?

Arriane flew low to the ground, seeking small signs. At various points she would see spots of blood on blades of tall grass, but then she would lose the trail again. At one point, having crossed a creek bed, the trail disappeared completely, and Arriane wailed, feeling all was lost.

But then, near a weeping willow tree, she picked up her lover's path again.

Blood streamed for twenty yards—the trail widened and had splashed far, as if a fresh wound had been inflicted. Was an enemy hunting Tess, wounding her as she fled? Arriane sped up, desperate to come between Tess and whatever evil would dare harm her.

Only one being could have hunted down a fully empowered demon. In her darkest imaginings, Arriane could see Lucifer, the layers of cataracts on his eyes, his tremendous wings sprawling with rank black hairs.

But would Lucifer have come here, to wrestle Tess back to Hell? Arriane had never seen her love face to face with her master, though visions of it haunted her. If she discovered Lucifer in the act of harming Tess, Arriane didn't know what she would do. She could barely fly through the rage that was building inside.

Love like this was fatal, even for an angel.

"Tessriel!" she bellowed again into the endless fields of green. But she heard nothing.

In the west, storm clouds formed a dirty screen across the sky. Arriane hoped that Tess hadn't traveled in that direction. Everything about the rain—its scent, its effect on the terrain, its purifying quality—would throw Arriane off the trail.

But maybe Tess was counting on that very thing.

So the heart of the tempest was where she would go.

Arriane flattened her wings. She focused on picking up velocity. Turbulence shook her. Her body rocked from left to right, up and down, until she was soaked and shivering and spitting rain.

That was when she saw Tess, lying on her back at the edge of a stony promontory in the foothills of the Dolomites, not far from where Arriane had first sensed that something was terribly wrong.

Tess looked like she was *dying*—but angels did not die. Her wings flailed out unnaturally on either side of her. Blood streamed from them, pooling on a flat rock beneath her. She was alone.

She was *alone*.

Arriane was a hundred feet above her in the air, but the dull silver gleam in Tess's hand was unmistakable.

But why would Tess possess a starshot?

Arriane dipped down so quickly the wind roared in her ears. She landed on a light-gray boulder a few feet in front of Tess. Her wings cast a circle of light in front of her, enfolding Tess's body in a cool halo of illumination. It was easy to see now: The starshot had lacerated the demon's left wing. It wasn't completely severed, but the formerly powerful copper wing now hung by the thinnest strand of empyreal fibers.

Rage flashed through Arriane—she would murder whoever had done this. Then she looked at Tess's ashen face, eyes barely open, gazing up at her.

And she understood.

There was no one else to blame. This harshest of all wounds was self-inflicted.

Only hours earlier, Arriane had been thinking about the purity of an angel's skin, how nothing ever left a mark. But it wasn't absolutely true—some things left permanent scars.

Lucifer could do it with the ink of his tattoos.

A starshot wound could do it—if it did not kill the angel.

The mingling of—

"Tessriel, no!"

The demon held the starshot in her right hand and drew it near the wound again, as if intent on amputating the gilded wing from her body. But her fingers trembled so badly that the starshot sliced into other sections of the wing, spewing blood from its muscle-thick center. Only then did she seem to register Arriane's presence.

"You've come back." Her voice was as thin as the mountain air.

"Oh, Tessriel." Arriane's hands covered her heart. "They will never heal from this."

"That is the idea. I needed something to remember you by."

"Don't say that." Arriane dropped to her knees, crawling to where Tess lay upon the ground. "What were you even doing with a starshot? Bartering with Azazel? That isn't done!"

"It is done when the need is great enough. If I cannot have you, I do not want anything at all." Tess grimaced as she thrust the starshot in a downward slicing motion across her mutilated wing. It made a sound like flesh being ripped apart, but it did not sever the wing completely. "It is harder than you think."

"Stop it!" Arriane yelled, shooting out her hand to grab the starshot from Tess.

In a flash, Tess turned the starshot on her. "Stay back," she said weakly. "You know what will happen if you touch me."

Arriane studied the fallen angel she loved, covered in the blood that—if she touched it—would work like poison against her.

But even knowing that didn't stop Arriane. She needed Tess to know that she was not alone, that she was loved.

The memory of Tess laughing echoed in her ears and warmed her insides; the image of Tess, dear, sweet, beautiful Tess, played across Arriane's eyes as she did the unthinkable:

She lunged toward Tessriel, throwing herself on top of the demon, grabbing for the starshot, crying out in anguish as Tessriel's blood seared her. It was the singular pain of demon blood on angel flesh, like a thousand dull swords driving into her soul.

Blood on blood was even worse.

Arriane gritted her teeth, nearly going mad with the pain as she wrested the starshot from Tess's hand.

"Let me go!" Tess's fingernails tore at Arriane's throat until they broke the skin and Arriane's own blood began to flow. An animalistic howl left Arriane's lips.

Her blood actually boiled as it met Tessriel's, turning

to acid on her body and singeing off her skin. Wherever their blood commingled, bubbles rose up on the left side of her body, ugly scars knotting up her leg and torso and neck.

Still Arriane did not let go.

"Now see what you've done." Tess's lips were blue from losing so much blood. Sadistic laughter punctuated her anguish. "Even my blood is anathema to yours, and yours to mine. Just like"—here her voice faltered and her eyes began to drift—"just like they always said."

"Stay still!" Arriane tried to focus beyond the acidic burning; the only thing that mattered was stanching the flow of Tess's blood. She weighed the two limp wings in her hands, not knowing what to do.

"You're making it worse!" Tess shrieked.

"Stop! You've lost too much blood already."

Tess was convulsing, but she steadied one hand on the rock and raised her head just enough to stare deep into Arriane's eyes. "You have broken my heart, Arriane. You cannot be the one who heals me."

Arriane's lip quivered. "I can. I will."

She tore at the skirt of her dairymaid's gown, using her teeth to rip the flimsy fabric into shreds. *It will never work,* she thought as she wove and stretched the fabric into a clumsy sling, draping it carefully around Tess's gushing left wing.

She quickly wove another sling, working until her

fingers were numb with cold and fear. Tess's body continued to seize, but her eyes were closed, and she did not respond to Arriane's admonitions to wake up.

These slings would not do. Tess's wounds needed celestial intervention. That would require Gabbe's help, and Gabbe would be furious—but she was Gabbe, so she would help anyway. Tess's wings would never be the same, but maybe someday she could fly.

It was only after Arriane had bandaged Tess's wings as best she could manage that she looked down at her own body. It was a miserable tableau.

Her neck blazed with pain. Her dress had fallen to pieces along the left side. Her skin was mottled with swirling blood and silver pus and flaking angel tissue. She had nothing to dress her wounds. She had used all of the cloth for Tess.

She fell across the demon's lap and sobbed. She needed help but could not carry Tess in her burned and battered state. What good would it do, anyway?

Maybe Tess was right: When one lover suffered from a broken heart, no matter how badly the other wanted to help, she couldn't be the one to heal it.

As far as possible, Arriane realized, each soul had to be content alone before plunging into love, because one never knew when the other would move out of that love. It was the greatest paradox: Souls need each other, but they also need to not need each other.

"I have to go," she whispered to Tess, whose breath was shallow, labored. "I will send help for you. Someone will come to take care of you.

"I love you and will never love another. The best way I can honor that is to go now and fight for the kind of love we shared, the kind of love I believe in. I hope someday you find what you are looking for." A tear slid down Arriane's cheek. "Happy Valentine's Day, my one and only."

A shooting star danced in a bright arc across the sky. North—just the direction Arriane would need to fly to find Daniel and Lucinda. Her neck throbbed when she rose from the rock, but despite her injuries, her wings felt powerful and pristine. She spread them wide and flew away.

ENDLESS LOVE

THE VALENTINE OF
DANIEL AND LUCINDA

ONE

LOVE LONG AGO

Luce found herself at the far end of a narrow alley under a slit of sun-bleached sky.

"Bill?" she whispered.

No reply.

She'd come out of the Announcer groggy and disoriented. Where was she now? There was a bustling brightness at the other end of the alley, some sort of busy market where Luce caught flashes of fruit and fowl changing hands.

A biting winter wind had frozen the puddles in the

alley into slush, but Luce was sweating in the black ball gown she wore . . . where had she first put on this tattered gown? The king's ball at Versailles. She'd found this dress in some princess's armoire. And then she'd kept it on when she stepped through to the performance of *Henry VIII* in London.

She sniffed at her shoulder: It still smelled like smoke from the fire that had burned down the Globe.

From above her came a set of loud bangs: shutters being thrown wide. Two women poked their heads out of adjacent second-story casement windows. Startled, Luce pressed herself against a shadowed wall to listen, watching as the women fussed about with a shared clothesline.

"Will you let Laura watch the festivities?" said one, a matronly woman in a simple gray cowl as she pinned an enormous pair of damp trousers to the line.

"I see no harm in *watching*," said the other, a younger woman. She shook out a dry linen shirt and folded it with swift efficiency. "So long as she doesn't partake of those bawdy displays. Cupid's Urn! Hah! Laura's only seen twelve years; she's far too young to fetch a broken heart!"

"Ah, Sally"—the other woman sighed through a thin smile—"you're too strict. Saint Valentine's is a day for all hearts, young *and* old. It might do you and the mister a bit of good to be swept up in its romance yourselves, eh?"

A lone peddler, a short man dressed in a blue tunic and blue tights, turned down the alley, pushing a wooden cart. The women eyed him with suspicion and lowered their voices.

"Pears," he sang up to the open casements, from which the women's heads and hands had disappeared. "Rotund fruit of love! A pear for your Valentine will make this next year a sweet one."

Luce edged along the wall toward the alley's exit. Where was Bill? She hadn't realized just how much she'd come to rely on the little gargoyle. She needed different clothes. An idea of where and when she was. And a briefing on what she was doing here.

Medieval city of some sort. A Valentine's Day festival. Who knew it was such an old tradition?

"Bill!" she whispered. But there was still no answer.

She reached the corner and edged her head around.

The sight of a soaring castle made her halt. It was massive and majestic. Ivory towers rose into the blue sky. Golden banners, each emblazoned with a lion, billowed gently from high poles. She half expected to hear a blare of trumpets. It was like stumbling accidentally upon a fairy tale.

Instinctively, Luce wished Daniel were there. This was the kind of beauty that didn't seem real until you shared it with someone you loved.

But there was no sign of Daniel. Just a girl.

A girl Luce recognized instantly.

One of her past selves.

Luce watched as the girl strolled across the cobble-stoned bridge that led to the tall doors of the castle. She moved past them, to the entrance of a fantastic rose garden, where the blossomless bushes were sculpted into tall, wall-like hedges. Her hair was loose and long and messy, trailing halfway down the back of her white linen gown. The old Luce—Lucinda—gazed longingly at the garden gate.

Then Lucinda stood on tiptoe, reached a pale hand over the gate, and from the middle of a bare-branched bush, bent the stem of a single unlikely red rose toward her nose.

Was it possible to smell a rose sadly? Luce couldn't say; all she knew was that something about this girl—herself—felt *sad*. But why? Did it have something to do with Daniel?

Luce was about to step fully from the shadowed alley when she heard a voice and saw a figure approach her past self.

"There you are."

Lucinda released the rose, which snapped back into the garden, losing its blossom on the thorns as it crossed. The red teardrop-shaped petals showered down on her shoulders as she turned to face the voice.

Luce watched Lucinda's posture change, a smile stretching across her face at the sight of Daniel. And

Luce felt that same smile on her *own* face. Their bodies might be different, their daily lives looked nothing alike, but when it came to Daniel, their shared soul aligned completely.

He wore a full suit of armor, though his helmet was off and his golden hair was lank with sweat and dirt. He'd clearly come from the road; the speckled white mare beside him looked weary. Luce had to fight every urge in her body not to run into his arms. He was breathtaking: a knight in shining armor to outshine any fairytale knight.

But this Daniel wasn't her Daniel. This Daniel belonged to another girl.

"You came back!" Lucinda broke into a run, her tresses streaming in the wind.

Her past self's arms stretched out, inches from Daniel—

But the image of her valiant knight wavered in the wind.

And then it was gone. Disgust crept into Luce's stomach as she watched Daniel's horse and armor vanish into thin air and Lucinda—who could not stop herself in time—crash headfirst into a belching stone gargoyle.

"Fumble!" Bill cackled, spinning in a loop-the-loop.

Lucinda screamed, tripped over her gown, and landed in the mud on her hands and knees. Bill's craggy laughter echoed off the façade of the castle. He flitted higher in the air and then eyed Luce glaring at him from across the street.

"There you are!" he said, cartwheeling toward her.

"I told you never to do that again!"

"My acrobatics?" Bill hopped onto her shoulder. "But if I do not practice, I win no medals," he said in a Russian accent.

She swatted him off. "I meant changing into Daniel."

"I didn't do it to you, I did it to her. Maybe your past self thinks it's funny."

"She doesn't."

"That's not my fault. Besides, I'm not a mind reader. You expect me to realize you're speaking on behalf of all Lucindas ever, every time you talk. You never said anything about not razzing your past lives. It's all in good fun. For me, anyway."

"It's *cruel*."

"If you insist on splitting hairs, fine, she's all yours. I suppose you don't need me pointing out that what *you* do with 'em ain't exactly humane!"

"You're the one who taught me how to go three-D."

"My point exactly," he said with an eerie cackle that sent goose bumps running up Luce's arms.

Bill's eyes fell on a diminutive stone gargoyle capping one of the columns of the garden gates. He banked in the air, circled back to the column, and slung his arm around the gargoyle's shoulder as if he'd finally found a true companion. "Mortals! Can't live with 'em, can't consign them to the fiery depths of Hell. Am I right or am I right?" He looked back at Luce. "Not a big talker."

Luce could no longer stand it. She ran forward, hurrying to help Lucinda up from the ground. Her past self's dress was torn at the knees and her face was sickly pale.

"Are you all right?" Luce asked. She expected the girl to be thankful, but instead, she recoiled.

"Who— What are you?" Lucinda gaped at Luce. "And what kind of devil is that thing?" She flung her hand in Bill's direction.

Luce sighed. "He's just— Don't worry about him."

Bill probably did look like a devil to this medieval incarnation. Luce most likely didn't look much better— some mental girl running up to her dressed in a futuristic ball gown that reeked of smoke?

"I'm sorry," Luce said, glancing over the girl's shoulder at Bill, who seemed amused.

"Thinking about going three-D?" Bill asked.

Luce cracked her knuckles. Fine. She knew she had to cleave to this past body if she was going to move forward on her quest, but there was something in her past self's face—bewilderment and a hint of inexplicable betrayal—that made her hesitate. "This, uh, this will just take a moment."

Her past self's eyes widened, but as she was about to pull away, Luce seized her past self's hand and squeezed.

The solid stones beneath her feet shifted and the world before Luce swirled like a kaleidoscope. Her stomach lurched up toward her throat, and as the world flattened back out, she was left with the distinctive nausea of cleaving. She blinked and, for that one unsettling instant, saw the disembodied view of both girls. There was medieval Lucinda—innocent, captive, and terrified; and there, beside her, was Luce—guilty, exhausted, obsessed.

There was no time to regret it. On the other side of the blink—

A single body, one conflicted soul.

And Bill's fat-lipped smirk taking it all in.

Luce clutched her heart through the rough linen dress Lucinda had been wearing. It hurt. Her whole body had become a heartache.

She was channeling Lucinda now, feeling what Lucinda had been feeling before Luce inhabited her body. It was a move that had become second nature to her—from Russia to Tahiti to Tibet—but no matter how many times she did it, Luce didn't think she'd ever get used to suddenly *feeling* so keenly the landscape of her past emotions.

Right now it was the kind of raw pain Luce hadn't experienced since her early days at Sword & Cross, when she loved Daniel so much she thought it might split her in two.

"You're looking a little green around the gills." Bill floated before her face, sounding more satisfied than concerned.

"It's my past. She's—"

"Panicked? Sick at heart with love for that worthless oaf of a knight? Yeah, the Daniel of this era jerked you around like a slot-machine pull on Seniors' Day at the casino." He crossed his arms broodingly over his chest and did something Luce had never seen before: He made his eyes flash violet. "Maybe I'll be at the Valentine's Faire," he said in a husky, affected tone, a grossly over-simplified impersonation of Daniel. "Or maybe I have better things to do, like slash losers with my humungous sword—"

"Don't do that, Bill." Luce shook her head, annoyed. "Besides, if Daniel doesn't show at this Valentine's thing, he's got a good reason—I'm sure of it."

"Yeah." The croak returned to Bill's voice. "You always are."

"He's trying to protect me," she argued, but her voice was weak.

"Or himself . . ."

Luce rolled her eyes. "Okay, Bill, what is it I'm sup-posed to learn in this lifetime? That you think Daniel's a jerk? Got it. Can we move on?"

"Not exactly."

Bill flew to the ground and sat beside her. "Actually, we're taking a holiday from your education in this life," he said. "Based on your snippiness and the bags under my eyes"—he stretched out and displayed a wrinkly fold of saggy skin, which made a sound like a shaken bag of marbles—"I'd say we both need a day off.

"So here's the deal: It's Valentine's Day—or an early form of it, anyway. Daniel is a knight, which means he's got his pick of the parties. He can grace the endless church-sanctioned nobleman's feast in the castle of his lord." Bill jerked his head toward the towering white turrets behind them. "Sure, there'll be a nice roast stag, maybe even a sprinkle of salt, but you've got to hang with the *clergy,* and whose idea of a party is that?"

Luce glanced back at the fairy-tale castle. That was where Daniel lived? Was he inside those walls now?

"Or," Bill continued, "he can slum it at the *real* party out on the green tonight for that less-respectable sort of folk, where the ale flows like wine and the wine flows like ale. There'll be dancing, dining, and most importantly, wenching."

"Wenching?"

Bill waved one tiny hand in the air. "Nothing you have to worry about, darlin'. Daniel only has eyes for one wench in all of creation. I mean you."

"Wench," Luce said, looking down at her rough-spun cotton garments.

"There's a certain lost wench"—Bill elbowed Luce—"who will be there at the Faire, scanning the crowd through the eyeholes of her painted mask for her hunky dreamboat." He patted her cheek. "Doesn't that sound like a great time, little sister?"

"I'm not here to have fun, Bill."

"Try it out for one night—who knows, you might enjoy it. Most people do."

Luce swallowed. "But what will happen when he finds me? What am I supposed to learn before I burn up, before—"

"Whoa there!" Bill cried. "Slow down, hothead. I told you—tonight's just about fun. A little bit of romance. A night off"—he winked—"for both of us."

"What about the curse? How can I drop everything and celebrate Valentine's Day?"

Bill didn't respond immediately. Instead, he paused thoughtfully, then said, "What if I told you that this—tonight—is the only Valentine's Day you kids ever got to spend together?"

The words struck Luce immediately. "Ever? We . . . never got to celebrate Valentine's Day?"

Bill shook his head. "After today? No."

Luce thought back to her days at Dover, how she and Callie would watch some of the other girls get chocolate hearts and roses on Valentine's Day. They'd made a tradition of lamenting how very, very single they were over strawberry milk shakes at the local diner. They'd spent hours conjecturing on the slim odds of ever having a date on Valentine's Day.

She laughed. She hadn't been far off: Luce had never had a Valentine's Day with Daniel.

Now Bill was telling her that she only ever had tonight.

Luce's quest through the Announcers, all her efforts to break the curse and discover what lay behind all of her reincarnations, finding an end to this endless cycle—yes, those were important. Of course they were.

But would the world end if she enjoyed this *one* time with Daniel?

She cocked her head at Bill. "Why are you doing this for me?" she asked.

Bill shrugged. "I have a heart, a soft spot for—"

"What? *Valentine's Day?* Why don't I buy that?"

"Even I once loved and lost." And for the briefest of moments, it seemed the gargoyle looked wistful and sad. He stared right at her and sniffled.

Luce gave a laugh. "Okay," she said. "I'll stay. Just for tonight."

"Good." Bill popped up and pointed a crooked claw down the alley. "Now go, make merry." He squinted. "Actually, change your dress. *Then* make merry."

TWO

A SOUL AT ODDS

Hours later, Luce leaned her elbows on the sill of the small stone casement window.

The village looked different from this second-story perch—a maze of interconnected stone buildings, thatched roofs angled here and there in something like a medieval apartment complex.

By late that afternoon, many of the windows, including the one Luce leaned out of, were draped with deep-green vines of ivy or dense boughs of holly that had been woven into wreaths. They were signs of the Faire taking place outside the city that evening.

Valentine's Day, Luce thought. She could feel Lucinda dreading it.

After Bill had disappeared outside the castle, for his mysterious "night off," things had happened very quickly: She'd wandered alone through the city until a girl a few years older than her appeared from nowhere to whisk Luce up a flight of dank stairs into this small two-roomed house.

"Draw away from the window, sister," a high voice called across the room. "You're letting in Saint Valentine's draft!"

The girl was Helen, Lucinda's older sister, and the smoky, confining two-roomed house was where she and her family lived. The chamber's gray walls were bare, and the only furniture consisted of a wooden bench, a trestle table, and the stack of family sleeping pallets. The floor was strewn with rough straw and sprinkled with lavender—a meager attempt to clear the air of the foul smell from the tallow candles they had to use for light.

"In a moment," Luce called back. The tiny window was the only place she didn't feel claustrophobic.

Down the alley to the right was the marketplace she'd glimpsed before, and if she leaned out far enough, she could see a sliver of the white stone castle.

It haunted Lucinda, that tiniest tease of a view—Luce

sensed this through the soul they shared—because on the evening of the day Lucinda first met Daniel in the rose garden, she'd come home and coincidentally seen him peering pensively out of the tallest tower casement. Since then, she watched for him every chance she got, but he never appeared again.

Another voice whispered: "What does she stare at for so long? What could possibly be so interesting?"

"The good Lord only knows," Helen replied, sighing. "My sister is laden with dreams."

Luce turned around slowly. Her body had never felt so strange. The part that belonged to medieval Lucinda was wilted and lethargic, flattened by the love she was certain she had lost. The part that belonged to Lucinda Price was holding fast to the idea that there might still be a chance.

It was a struggle to perform the simplest of tasks— like conversing with the three girls standing before her, alarmed expressions twisting their pretty faces.

The tallest one, in the middle, was Helen, Lucinda's only sister and the oldest of five children in their family. She was newly a wife, and as if to prove it, her thick blond hair was divided into two braids and pinned in a matronly chignon.

At Helen's side was Laura, their young neighbor, who Luce realized was the girl she'd overheard the two women gossiping about over the clothesline. Though

Laura was only twelve, she was alluringly beautiful—blond with large blue eyes and a loud, saucy laugh that could be heard across the city.

Luce bit back a laugh, trying to reconcile Laura's mother's protectiveness with what Lucinda knew of the girl's own experience—pressing palms with the page boys in the cool recesses of the lord's wood. What Luce gleaned from Lucinda's memories of Laura reminded her of Arriane. Laura, like the angel, was easy to love.

Then there was Eleanor, Lucinda's oldest, closest friend. They'd grown up wearing one another's clothes, like sisters. They bickered like sisters, too. Eleanor had a blunt edge, often slicing dreamy Lucinda's reveries in two with a cutting remark. But she had a skill for bringing Lucinda back to reality, and she loved Lucinda deeply. It wasn't, Luce realized, so different from her present-day relationship with Shelby.

"Well?" Eleanor asked.

"Well, what?" Lucinda said, startled. "Don't all stare at me at once!"

"We've only asked you three times which mask you're going to wear tonight." Eleanor waved three brightly colored masks in Lucinda's face. "Pray, end the suspense!"

They were simple leather domino masks, made to cover just the eyes and nose and tie around the back of the head with thin silk ribbon. All three were covered in the same coarse fabric, but each had been painted with a different design: one red with small black pansies, one green with delicate white blossoms, and one ivory with pale pink roses near the eyes.

"She stares as if she has not seen these same masks every one of her past five years of masquerading!" Eleanor murmured to Helen.

"She has the gift of seeing old things anew," Helen said.

Luce shivered, though the room was warmer than it had been for most of the winter months. In exchange for the eggs the citizens had offered as gifts to the lord, he'd repaid each household with a small bundle of cedar firewood. So the hearth was bright and cheery, giving a healthy flush to the girls' cheeks.

Daniel had been the knight tasked with collecting the eggs and distributing the firewood. He'd stridden through the door with purpose, then staggered back when he saw Lucinda inside. It was the last time medieval Lucinda had seen him, and after months of stolen moments together in the forest, Luce's past self was certain she would never see Daniel again.

But why? Luce wondered now.

Luce felt Lucinda's shame at her family's meager accommodations—but that didn't seem right. Daniel wouldn't care that Lucinda was a peasant's daughter. He knew that she was always and ever much more than that. There had to be something else. Something Lucinda was too sad to see clearly. But Luce could help her—find Daniel, win him back, at least for as long as she still had to live.

"I like the ivory one for you, Lucinda," Laura prompted, trying to be helpful.

But Luce could not make herself care about the masks. "Oh, any of them will be fine. Perhaps the ivory to match my gown." She tugged dully at the draped fabric of her worn wool dress.

The girls erupted into laughter.

"You're not going to wear *that* common market gown?" Laura gasped. "But we're all getting done up in our finest!" She collapsed dramatically across the wooden bench near the hearth. "Oh, I would never want to fall in love wearing my dreary Tuesday kirtle!"

A memory pushed to the front of Luce's mind: Lucinda had disguised herself as a lady in her one fine gown and sneaked into the castle rose garden. That was where she first met Daniel in this life. That was why their romance felt like a betrayal from the beginning. Daniel had thought Lucinda something other than a peasant's daughter.

That was why the thought of donning that fine red gown again and pretending to make merry at a festival was a staggering prospect to Lucinda.

But Luce knew Daniel better than Lucinda did. If he had an opportunity to spend Valentine's Day with her, he would seize it.

Of course, she could explain none of this inner turmoil to the girls. All she could do was turn away and subtly wipe her tears with the back of her wrist.

"She looks as if love has already found and dealt roughly with her," Helen murmured under her breath.

"I say, if love is rough with you, be rough with love!" Eleanor said in her bossy way. "Stamp out sadness with dancing slippers!"

"Oh, Eleanor," Luce heard herself say. "You wouldn't understand."

"And you *do* understand?" Eleanor laughed. "You, the girl who wouldn't even put her name in Cupid's Urn?"

"Oh, Lucinda!" Laura cupped her hands over her mouth. "Why not? I'd give anything if Mother would let me put my name in Cupid's Urn!"

"Which is why *I* had to toss her name into the urn for her!" Eleanor cried, seizing the train of Luce's gown and pulling her around the room in a circle.

After a chase that toppled the bench and the tallow candle on the casement ledge, Luce grabbed Eleanor's hand. "You didn't!"

"Oh, a little fun will do you good! I want you dancing tonight, high and lively with the rest of the maskers.

Come now, help me choose a visor. Which color makes my nose look smaller, rose or green? Perhaps I shall trick a man into loving me yet!"

Luce's cheeks were burning. Cupid's Urn! How did that have anything to do with a Valentine's Day with Daniel?

Before she could speak, out came Lucinda's party dress—a floor-length gown of red wool adorned with a narrow collar made of otter fur. It was cut lower across the chest than anything Luce would wear back home in Georgia; if Bill were here to see her, he would probably grunt a "Hubba hubba" in her ear.

Luce sat still while Helen's fingers wove a stem of holly berries into her loose black hair. She was thinking of Daniel, the way his eyes had lit up in the rose garden when he first approached Lucinda. . . .

A rapping startled them all; in the doorway, a woman's face appeared. Luce recognized her instantly as Lucinda's mother.

Without thinking, she ran into the safe warmth of her mother's arms.

They closed around her shoulders, tight and affectionate. It was the first of the lives Luce had visited where she felt a strong connection with her mother. It made her feel blissful and homesick all at once.

Back home in Thunderbolt, Georgia, Luce tried to act mature and self-sufficient as often as she could.

Lucinda was just the same, Luce realized. But at times like this—when heartbreak made the whole world cheerless—nothing would do but the comfort of a mother's embrace.

"My daughters, so fine and grown up, you make me feel older than I am!" Their mother laughed as she ran her fingers through Luce's hair. She had kind hazel eyes and a soft, expressive brow.

"Oh, Mother," Luce said with her cheek against her mother's shoulder. She was thinking of Doreen Price and trying not to cry.

"Mother, tell us again how you met Father at the Valentine's Faire," Helen said.

"Not that old tale again!" Their mother groaned, but the girls could see the story forming in her eyes already.

"Yes! Yes!" the girls all chanted.

"Why, I was younger than Lucinda when I was a mother made," her willowy voice began. "My own mother bade me wear the mask she'd worn years before. She gave me this advice on my way out the door: 'Smile, child, men like a happy maid. Seek happy nights to happy days . . .'"

As her mother dove into her tale of love, Luce found her eyes creeping back toward the casement, imagining the turrets of the castle, the vision of Daniel looking out. Looking for her?

After her story was done, her mother drew something

from the pocket strung around her waist and handed it to Luce with a mischievous wink.

"For you," she whispered.

It was a small cloth package tied with twine. Luce went to the window and carefully unwrapped it. Her fingers trembled as she loosened the twine.

Inside was a lacy heart-shaped doily about the size of her fist. Someone had inscribed these words with what looked to Luce like a blue Bic pen:

> *Roses are red,*
> *Violets are blue,*
> *Sugar is sweet,*
> *And so are you.*
> *I will look for you tonight—*
> *Love, Daniel*

Luce almost sputtered with laughter. This was something the Daniel she knew would *never* write. Clearly, someone else had been behind it. Bill?

But to the part of Luce that was Lucinda, the words were a chaos of scribbles. She couldn't read, Luce realized. And yet, once the meaning of the poem was processed by Luce, she could feel an understanding break open in Lucinda. Her past self found this the freshest, most captivating poetry ever known.

She would go to the festival and she would find

Daniel. She would show Lucinda how powerful their love could be.

Tonight there would be dancing. Tonight there would be magic in the air. And—even if it was the only time it ever happened in the long history of Daniel and Lucinda—tonight there would be the particular joy of spending Valentine's Day with the one she loved.

THREE

DELIGHT IN DISORDER

"Eleanor!" Luce shouted over a dense crowd of dancers as her friend bounced past in the spirited line of a jig. But Eleanor didn't hear her.

It was hard to say whether Luce's voice was drowned out by the delighted hoots of a crowd at a puppet show in one of the movable stages set up on the western edge of the dancing area for the raucous, hungry crowd lining up at the long food tables on the eastern side of the green. Or maybe it was just the sea of dancers in the middle, who bounded, twirled, and spun with reckless, romantic abandon.

It seemed as though the dancers at the Valentine's Faire were not just dancing—but also hollering, laughing, belting out verses to the troubadour's music, and hollering to friends across the muddy dance area. They were doing it all at once. And all at the top of their lungs.

Eleanor was out of earshot, spinning as she stamped out dance steps all the way across the oak-ringed green. Luce had no choice but to turn back to her clumsy partner and curtsy.

He was a spindly older man with sallow cheeks and ill-fitting lips whose slouched shoulders made him look like he wanted to hide behind his too-small lynx-face mask.

And yet Lucinda didn't care. She couldn't remember ever having had this much fun dancing. They'd been dancing since the sun kissed the horizon; now the stars shone like armor in the sky. There were always so many stars in past skies. The night was chilly, but Luce's face was flushed and her forehead was damp with perspiration. As the song neared its end, she thanked her partner and sidled between a line of dancers, eager to get away.

Because despite the joys of dancing under the stars, Luce hadn't forgotten about the real reason she was here.

She looked out across the green and worried that

even if Daniel was somewhere out there, she might never find him. Four troubadours dressed in motley gathered on a wobbly dais at the northern edge of the green, plucking on lutes and lyres to play a song as sweet as a Beatles ballad. At a high school dance, these slow songs were the ones that made the single girls, including Luce, a little anxious—but here, the moves were built into the songs and no one was ever at a loss for a partner. You just grabbed the nearest warm body, for better or for worse, and you danced. A skipping jig for this one, a circling dance in groups of eight for another. Luce felt Lucinda knowing some of the moves innately; the rest of them were easy to pick up.

If only Daniel were here . . .

Luce withdrew to the edge of the green, taking a break. She studied the women's dresses. By modern standards, they weren't fancy, but the women wore them with such pride that the dresses seemed as elegant as any of the fine gowns she'd seen at Versailles. Many were made of wool; a few had linen or cotton accents sewn into a collar or a hem. Most people in the city only owned one pair of shoes, so worn leather boots abounded, but Luce quickly realized how much easier it was to dance in them than in high-heeled shoes that pinched her feet.

The men managed to look dapper in their best breeches. Most wore a long wool tunic on top for warmth. Hoods were tossed back over their shoulders—

the weather that night was above freezing, almost mild. Most of their leather masks were painted to mimic the faces of forest animals, complementing the floral designs of the ladies' masks. A few men wore gloves, which looked expensive. But most of the hands Luce touched that night were cold and chapped and red.

Cats stared from dirt roads around the green. Dogs searched for their owners among the mess of bodies. The air smelled like pine and sweat and beeswax candles and the sweet musk of fresh-baked gingerbread.

As the next song wound down, Luce spotted Eleanor, who seemed happy to be plucked from the arm of a boy whose red mask was painted like a fox's face.

"Where's Laura?"

Eleanor pointed toward a stand of trees, where their young friend leaned close to a boy they didn't recognize, whispering something. He was showing her a book, gesturing in the air. It looked like he took a great deal of care with his hair. He wore a mask made to resemble a rabbit's face.

The girls shared a giggle as they made their way through the crowd. There was Helen, sitting with her husband on a wool blanket spread out on the grass. They were sharing a wooden cup of steaming cider and laughing easily about something, which made Luce miss Daniel all over again.

There were lovers everywhere. Even Lucinda's parents had turned out for the Faire. Her father's wiry white beard scraped her mother's cheek as they sashayed around the green.

Luce sighed, then fingered the lace doily in her pocket.

Roses are red, violets are blue, if Daniel didn't write these words, then who?

The last time she'd received a note allegedly from Daniel, it had been a trap set by the Outcasts—

And Cam had saved her.

Heat rose on the back of her neck. Was this a trap? Bill had said it was just a Valentine's party. He'd put so much energy into helping her on her quest already, he wouldn't have left her alone like this if there had been any real danger. Right?

Luce shook the thought away. Bill had said Daniel would be here, and Luce believed him. But the wait was killing her.

She followed Eleanor toward a long table, where plates and bowls of casual, pot-luck-style food had been set out. There were sliced duck served over cabbage, whole hares that had been roasted on spits, cauldrons of baby cauliflowers with a bright orange sauce, high-piled platters of apples, pears, and dried currants harvested from the surrounding forests, and a whole long wooden table filled with misshapen, half-burned pies of meat and fruit.

She watched a man loosen a flat knife from a strap slung around his waist and cut himself a hefty slice of pie. On her way out the door that evening, Luce's mother had handed her a shallow wooden spoon, which she had threaded through a wool tie around her waist. These people were prepared for eating, fixing, and fighting, the way Luce was prepared for love.

Eleanor reappeared at Luce's side and held a bowl of porridge under her nose.

"Gooseberry jam on top," Eleanor said. "Your favorite."

When Luce dipped her spoon into the thick concoction, a savory aroma wafted up and made her mouth water. It was hot and hearty and delicious—exactly what she needed to revive her for another dance. Before she realized it, she had eaten it all.

Eleanor glanced down at the empty bowl, surprised. "Danced up an appetite, did you?"

Luce nodded, feeling warm and satisfied. Then she noticed two brown-robed clergymen sitting apart from the crowd on a wooden bench beneath an elm tree. Neither was taking part in the festivities—in fact, they looked more like chaperones than revelers—but the younger one moved his feet in time with the rhythm, while the other, who had a shriveled-looking face, glared darkly at the crowds.

"The Lord sees and hears this lewd debauchery perpetrated so near His house," the shriveled-faced man scoffed.

"And closer than that, even." The other clergyman

laughed. "Do you recall, Master Docket, just how much of the church's gold went toward His Lordship's Valentine's banquet? Was it twenty gold pieces for that stag? These people's festivities cost nothing more than the energy to dance. And they dance like angels."

If only Luce could see her angel dancing toward her right now . . .

"Angels who'll sleep through tomorrow's working hours, mark my words, Master Herrick."

"Can you not see the joy on these young faces?" The younger vicar's eyes swept across the green, found Luce's at the edge of the lawn, and brightened.

She found herself smiling back behind her mask—but her joy that evening would be vastly increased if she could be there in Daniel's arms. Otherwise, what was the point of taking this romantic night off?

It seemed that Luce and the shriveled-faced vicar were the only two people here *not* relishing the masquerade. And generally Luce loved a good party, but right now all she wanted to do was pluck the masks off the face of every boy who passed. What if she'd already missed him in the crowd? How would she know if the Daniel of this era would even be looking for her?

She stared so baldly at a tall blond boy whose mask made him look like an eagle that he bounded past the toymaker's stall and the puppet show to stand before her.

"Shall I introduce myself, or would you rather just keep staring?" His teasing voice sounded neither familiar nor unfamiliar.

For a moment, Luce held her breath.

She imagined the ecstasy of his hands around her waist . . . the way he always dipped her backward to preface a kiss . . . She wanted to touch the place where his wings bloomed from his shoulders, the secret scar no one knew about but her . . .

When she reached up to lift his mask, the boy grinned at her boldness—but his smile faded as quickly as Luce's did when she saw his face.

He was perfectly good-looking; there was just one problem: He wasn't Daniel. And so every aspect of this boy—from his square nose, to his strong jaw, to his pure-gray eyes—paled in comparison to the boy she had in mind. She let out a long, sad sigh.

The boy couldn't hide his embarrassment. He fumbled for words, then slipped his mask back over his face, making Luce feel terrible.

"I'm sorry," she said, quickly backing away. "I mistook you for someone else."

Luckily, she backed into Laura, whose face, unlike Lucinda's, was cheery with the magic of the night.

"Oh, I hope they'll draw from Cupid's Urn soon!" Laura whispered, bouncing on her heels and drawing Luce mercifully away from the eagle boy.

"Did you sneak your name in there after all?" Luce asked, finding a smile.

Laura shook her head. "Mother would slaughter me!"

"Won't be much longer." Eleanor appeared at their side. She looked nervous. She was confident about everything except boys. "They draw at the toll of the next church bells, to give the new sweethearts a chance to dance. Perhaps a kiss if they're lucky."

The next church bells. To Luce, it seemed like the eight o'clock bells had only just rung, but she was certain time must be flying faster than she realized. Was it already almost nine? Her time to be with Daniel was running out—fast—and standing around obsessively scanning the gallery of masks wasn't doing any good. No eyes glowed violet behind their visor.

She had to act. Something told her she'd have better luck on the dance floor.

"Shall we dance again?" she asked the girls, pulling them back into the crowd.

❄

The revelers had stamped the grass into mud. The musical arrangement had grown more intricate, a quick waltz, and the dances had changed, too.

Luce followed the light, fast steps, picking up the more complicated arm movements as she went along.

Palm to palm with the gentleman in front of you, a simple curtsy, and then several skips in a wide circle around your partner to face the other side; then a swap with the girl to your left. Then palm to palm with the next young man, and the whole thing was repeated.

Halfway through the song, Luce was out of breath and giggling when she stopped in front of her new partner. Her feet suddenly felt welded to the mud.

He was tall and slender, wearing a mask with leopard's spots. The design was exotic to Lucinda—there were no leopards in the woods around her city. It was certainly the most elegant mask she'd seen at the party. The man extended his gloved hands, and when Luce slipped hers cautiously inside, his grip was firm, almost possessive. Behind the holes around the leopard's eyes, there came a gentle glow as emerald-green irises locked with hers.

FOUR

SOME CONSEQUENCE YET
HANGING IN THE STARS

"Good evening, lady. How nimbly you dance. Like an angel."

Luce's lips parted to respond, but her voice caught in her throat.

Why did Cam have to crash this party?

"Good evening, sir," Luce responded with a quiver in her voice. From all the dancing, her face was flushed, and her braids had tumbled loose, and one of the sleeves of her dress had slipped off her shoulder. She could feel

Cam's gaze on her bare skin. She reached to right her sleeve, but his gloved hand crossed hers to stop her.

"Such sweet disorder in your dress." He drew a finger across her collarbone and she shivered. "It inspires a man's imagination."

The song changed keys, a cue for the dancers to change partners. Cam's fingers lifted off her skin, but Luce's heart still pounded as they danced away from each other.

She watched Cam from the corner of her eye. He was watching her. She knew somehow that this was not Cam from the present chasing her backward through time. This was the Cam who lived and breathed in this medieval air.

He was easily the most elegant dancer on the green. There was an ethereal quality to his steps that did not go unnoticed by the ladies. From the attention he was getting, Luce knew he was not from this city. He'd arrived specially to attend the Valentine's Faire. But why?

Then they were paired again. Was she still dancing? Her body felt stiff and rigid. Even the music seemed to stutter in an endless in-between beat, which made Luce worry that she and Cam would have to stay rooted to these spots, staring into one another's eyes forever.

"Are you all right, sir?" Luce hadn't expected to say that. But there was something strange in his expression.

It was a darkness even his mask could not conceal.

This was not the dark of evil doings, not the terrifying way he'd appeared in the cemetery at Sword & Cross. No, this Cam's soul was crippled by sorrow.

What could make him look like that?

His eyes narrowed, as if he sensed her thoughts, and something in his face shifted.

"I have never been better." Cam tilted his head. "It's you I'm worried about, Lucinda."

"Me?" Luce tried hard not to show how he affected her. She wished for a different kind of mask altogether, an invisible one, which would prevent him from ever again thinking he knew how she felt.

He raised his mask to his forehead. "You're engaged in an impossible endeavor. You'll end up brokenhearted and alone. Unless—"

"Unless what?"

He shook his head. "There is so much darkness in you, Lucinda." The leopard mask lowered again. "Come back around, come back around. . . ."

His voice trailed off as he began to dance away. For once, Luce wasn't through with him. "Wait!"

But Cam had disappeared into the dance.

He was striding in slow circles with a new partner. Laura. Cam murmured something in the innocent girl's ear, and she tossed back her head and laughed. Luce fumed. She wanted to jerk simple, bright Laura away from Cam's darkness. She wanted to grab Cam and force him to explain. She wanted to have a conversation on her terms, not at momentary, melodramatic intervals between jig steps in the middle of a public festival in the Middle Ages.

There he was again, coming toward her in perfect control of the steps, as if influencing the tempo of the music. Luce couldn't have felt more out of control. Just when he was about to come before her again, a tall blond man dressed entirely in black deftly pushed him aside. He stood before her and made no pretense of dancing.

"Hello."

She sucked in her breath. "Hello."

Tall, muscular, mysterious beyond all possibility. She would know him anywhere. She reached for him, desperate to feel some connection, to feel the sweetest flush at the touch of her true love's skin—

Daniel.

Just as the music was about to dictate that they change partners, it slowed—almost like magic—and morphed into something slow and beautiful.

Flames from the candles positioned all around the Faire flickered against the dark sky, and the entire world seemed to hold its breath. Luce stared into Daniel's eyes, and all the movement and colors around him faded away.

She had found him.

His arms came toward her, circling her waist as her

body melted into his, buzzing with the thrill of his touch. Then she was deep in Daniel's arms and there was nothing so wonderful in all the world as dancing with her angel. Their feet kissed the ground with the lightness of their steps, and the flight was so obvious and innate in Daniel's body. She felt the buoyancy in her own heart, too, which she felt only when Daniel was near.

There was nothing so wonderful—except maybe his kiss.

Her lips parted in expectation, but Daniel just watched her, drinking her in with his eyes.

"I thought you'd never come," she said.

Luce thought about escaping through the Announcers in her backyard, about chasing down her past lifetimes and watching them burn up, about the fights she and Daniel had had over keeping her safe and alive. Sometimes it was easy to forget how good they were together. How lovely he was, how kind, the way being with him made her feel like she was flying.

Just looking at him made the tiny hairs on her arms stand up, made her stomach flip-flop with nervous energy. And that was nothing compared to what kissing him did to her.

He raised his mask and held her so tightly against him she couldn't move. She didn't want to. She pored over every lovely feature of his face, her eyes lingering the longest on the soft curve of his lips. After all this buildup, she simply couldn't believe it. It was really him!

"I will always come back to you." His eyes held her in a trance. "Nothing can stop me."

Luce rose on her toes, desperate to kiss him, but Daniel pressed a finger to her lips and smiled. "Come with me," he whispered, taking her hand.

Daniel led her past the edge of the green, past the ring of oak trees that encircled the revelers. The high grass tickled her ankles and the moon lit their way until they entered the chilly darkness of the forest. There Daniel picked up a small, glowing lantern, as if this was all part of his plan.

"Where are we going?" she asked, though it didn't really matter, as long as they were together.

Daniel just shook his head and smiled, holding out a hand to help her hop over a fallen branch blocking the path.

As they walked, the music faded until it was hard to discern, mingling with the low hooting of owls, the rustling of squirrels in tree branches, and the soft song of the nightingale. The lantern rocked on Daniel's arm and the light wobbled, reaching for the web of bare branches curling out toward them. Once, Luce would have been nervous about the shadows in the forest, but that seemed like millennia ago.

As they walked hand in hand, Luce's and Daniel's feet traced a narrow pebble path. The night grew colder and she leaned close to him for warmth, burrowing deep into the arms he wrapped around her.

When they arrived at a fork in the path, Daniel paused for a moment, almost as if he'd lost his way. Then he turned to face her. "I should explain," he said. "I owe you a Valentine's gift."

Luce laughed. "You don't owe me anything. I just want to be with you."

"Ah, but I received your gift—"

"*My* gift?" She looked up, surprised.

"And it touched me to my core." He reached out and took her hand. "I should apologize if I have ever made you wonder about my affections. Until just yesterday, I didn't think I would be able to meet you here tonight."

A crow cawed, soaring overhead and landing on a wobbly branch above them.

"But then a messenger arrived and gave all the knights in my care strict instructions to attend the Faire. I fear I rode my horse to near exhaustion in my haste to find you here tonight. It's just that I have been so eager to repay you for your most thoughtful gift."

"But Daniel, I didn't—"

"Thank you, Lucinda." Then he produced a leather sheath that looked like it might hold a dagger. Luce tried not to look too baffled, but she had never seen it before in her life.

"Oh." She laughed under her breath and fingered the doily in her pocket. "Do you ever get the feeling someone's watching over us?"

He smiled and said, "All the time."

"Maybe they're our guardian angels," Luce murmured jokingly.

"Maybe," Daniel said. "But happily, right now, I think it's just you and me."

He guided her to the left-hand path; they took a few more steps, then turned right and passed a crooked oak tree. In the darkness Luce could sense a small, circular clearing, where a vast oak tree must have been chopped down. Its stump stood in the center of the clearing—and something had been placed on it, but Luce couldn't see what yet.

"Close your eyes," he told her, and when she did, she sensed the lantern moving away. She heard him rustling around the clearing, and she came very close to peeking, but she managed to hold out, wanting to experience the surprise just the way Daniel had intended it.

After a moment, a familiar scent filled Luce's nose. She closed her eyes and inhaled deeply. Something soft, floral . . . and absolutely unmistakable.

Peonies.

Still standing with her eyes closed, Luce could see her dreary dorm room back at Sword & Cross, made beautiful by the vase of peonies in her window that Daniel had brought to her at the hospital. She could see the cliff's edge in Tibet, where she'd stepped through to witness Daniel doling out single flowers to her past self in a game that ended too soon. She could almost smell the gazebo in Helston, which teemed with the peonies' feathery white blooms.

"Now open your eyes."

She could hear the smile in Daniel's voice, and when she opened her eyes and saw him standing before the tree stump decked with a vast bouquet of peonies in a tall, wide copper vase, she covered her mouth and gasped. But that wasn't all. Daniel had threaded peony blossoms through the slender branches. He'd made vases of the pocks in all the surrounding trees' stumps. He'd strewn the ground with the peonies' delicate, snowy petals. He had woven a wreath for her hair. He'd lit dozens of candles in small hanging lanterns all around, so that the whole clearing glowed with a magical brilliance. When he stepped forward to place the wreath on Luce's head, she—and her medieval self—nearly melted.

Medieval Lucinda didn't recognize the vast array of flowers; she would have no idea how this was possible in February—and she still loved every inch of the surprise. But Lucinda Price knew that the pure-white peonies were more than just a Valentine's Day gift. They were the symbol of Daniel Grigori's eternal love.

The candlelight flickered on his face. He was smiling but looked nervous, as if he didn't know whether she liked his gift or not.

"Oh, Daniel." She raced into his arms. "They're beautiful."

He swung her in a circle and steadied the wreath on her head.

"They're called peonies. Not traditional Valentine's flowers," he said, tossing his head thoughtfully, "but still, they are . . . something of a tradition."

Luce loved that she understood exactly what he meant.

"Perhaps we could make them our Valentine's tradition," she suggested.

Daniel plucked a large blossom from the bouquet and slipped it between her fingers, holding it close to her heart. How many times across history had he done the exact same thing? Luce could see a glimmer in his eyes that suggested it never got old.

"Yes, our very own Valentine's tradition," he mused. "Peonies and . . . well, there ought to be something else. Oughtn't there?"

"Peonies and"—Luce racked her brain. She didn't need anything else. Didn't need anything but Daniel . . . and, well . . . "How about peonies and a kiss?"

"That's a very, very good idea."

Then he kissed her, his lips diving toward hers with unsurpassed desire.

The kiss felt wild and new and exploratory, as if they'd never kissed before.

Daniel was lost in the kiss, fingers woven through her hair, his breath hot on her neck as his lips explored her earlobes and her collarbone, the low cut of her dress.

Neither of them could get enough air, but they refused to stop kissing.

An itch of heat crept up Luce's neck, and her pulse began to race.

Was it happening?

She would die of love right here, in the middle of this glowing white forest. She didn't want to leave Daniel, didn't want to be cast into the sky, into another black hole with only Bill for a companion.

Damn this curse. Why was she bound to it? Why couldn't she break free?

Tears of frustration welled in her eyes. She pulled away from Daniel's lips, pressing her forehead to his and breathing hard, waiting for fire to sear her soul and take this body's life.

Only—when she stopped kissing Daniel, the heat faded, like a pot being lifted off a fire. She flew to his lips again.

The heat bloomed through her like a rose in summer.

But something was different. This was not the all-consuming flame that extinguished her, that had exiled her from past bodies and sent whole theaters up in smoke. This was the warm, dazzling ecstasy of kissing someone you truly loved—someone you were meant to be with forever. And for now.

Daniel watched her nervously, sensing that something important had happened inside her. "Is anything the matter?"

There was so much to say—

A thousand questions jockeyed for the tip of her tongue, but then a gruff voice jarred her imagination.

The only Valentine's Day you kids ever got to spend together.

How was that possible? So much love had passed between them, and yet they had never before spent or would never again spend the most famously romantic day of the year in each other's arms.

Yet here they were, stuck in a moment between past and future, bittersweet and precious, confusing and strange and incredibly alive. Luce didn't want to screw this up. Maybe Bill, and the kind young clergyman, and her dear friend Laura were each right in their way.

Maybe it was sweet enough just to be in love.

"Nothing's wrong. Just kiss me, and kiss me again and again."

Daniel lifted her off the ground and held her cradled in his arms. His lips were like honey. She wrapped her arms around the back of his neck. His hands traced the small of her back. Luce could barely breathe. She was overcome with love.

In the distance, church bells rang. They would be drawing from Cupid's Urn now, boys' hands randomly selecting their sweethearts, girls' cheeks red with anticipation, everyone hoping for a kiss. Luce closed her eyes and wished that every couple on the green—that every couple in the world—could share a kiss as sweet as this one.

"Happy Valentine's Day, Lucinda."

"Happy Valentine's Day, Daniel. Here's to many, many more."

He gave her a warm, hopeful look and nodded. "I promise."

EPILOGUE

THE GUARDIANS

Back on the green, four troubadours completed their last song and exited the stage to make room for the presentation of Cupid's Urn. As all the tittering single young men and women pressed excitedly up to the platform, the troubadours sneaked off to the side.

One by one, they raised their masks.

Shelby tossed down her recorder. Miles strummed one more chord on his lyre for good measure, and Roland harmonized on his fretted lute. Arriane slipped her hautboy into its slender wooden case and went to help herself to a big mug of punch. But she winced as she tossed it back and pressed a hand to the bloody cloth dressing the new wound on her neck.

"You jammed pretty well out there, Miles," Roland said. "You must have played the lyre somewhere before?"

"First time," Miles said nonchalantly, though it was clear he was pleased by the compliment. He glanced at Shelby and squeezed her hand. "I probably just sounded good because of Shel's accompaniment."

Shelby started to roll her eyes, but she only got halfway there before she gave up and leaned in to peck Miles softly on the lips. "Yeah, probably."

"Roland?" Arriane asked suddenly, spinning around to scan the green. "What happened to Daniel and Lucinda? A moment ago they were right over there. Oh"— she clapped her forehead—"can nothing go right for love?"

"We just saw them dancing," Miles said. "I'm sure they're okay. They're together."

"I told Daniel expressly, 'Spin Lucinda into the center of the green where we can see you.' It's as if he still doesn't know how much work goes into this!"

"I guess he had other plans," Roland said broodingly. "Love sometimes does."

"You guys, relax." Shelby's voice steadied the others,

as if her new love had bolstered her faith in the world. "I saw Daniel lead her into the forest, thataway. Stop!" she cried, tugging on Arriane's black cloak. "Don't follow them! Don't you think, after everything, they deserve some time alone?"

"Alone?" Arriane asked, letting out a heavy sigh.

"Alone." Roland came to stand next to Arriane, draping an arm around her, careful to avoid her injured neck.

"Yes," Miles said, his fingers threaded through Shelby's. "They deserve some time alone."

And in that moment under the stars, a simple understanding passed among the four. Sometimes love needed a lift from its guardian angels, to get its feet off the ground. But once it made its first early beats toward flight, it had to be trusted to take wing on its own and soar past the highest conceivable heights, into the heavens—and beyond.

RAPTURE

A FALLEN NOVEL

LAUREN KATE

THE FINAL BOOK IN THE FALLEN SERIES

Read on for a special preview.

RAPTURE

All other things to their destruction draw,

Only our love hath no decay. . . .

※ ※

—JOHN DONNE, *The Anniversary*

PROLOGUE

FALLING

First, there was silence—

In the space between Heaven and the Fall, deep in the unknowable distance, there was a moment when the glorious hum of Heaven disappeared and was replaced by a silence so profound that Daniel's soul strained to make out any noise.

Then came the actual feeling of falling—the kind of drop that even his wings couldn't save him from, as if the Throne had attached moons to them. They hardly beat, and when they did it made no impact on the trajectory of his fall.

Where was he going? There was nothing before him and nothing behind. Nothing up and nothing down. Only thick darkness, and the blurry outline of what was left of Daniel's soul.

In the absence of any noise whatsoever, his mind took over: It filled his head with something else, something inescapable: the haunting words of Luce's curse.

She will die. . . . She will never pass out of adolescence . . . will die again and again and again at precisely the moment when she remembers your choice.

You will never truly be together.

It was Lucifer's foul imprecation, his embittered addendum to the Throne's sentence passed there in the heavenly Meadow. Now death was coming for his love. Could Daniel stop it? Would he even recognize it?

For what did an angel know of death? Daniel had witnessed it come peacefully to some of the new mortal breeds called humans, but death was not the concern of angels.

Death and adolescence: the two absolutes in Lucifer's Curse. Neither meant a thing to Daniel. All he knew was that being separated from Lucinda was not a punishment he could endure. They had to be together.

"Lucinda!" he shouted.

His soul should have warmed at the very thought of her, but there was only aching absence.

He should have been able to sense his brethren around him—all of those who'd chosen wrongly or too late; who'd made no choice at all and been cast out for their indecision. He knew that he wasn't *truly* alone— more than one hundred million of them had plummeted when the ground beneath them opened up onto the void.

But he could neither see nor sense anyone else.

Before this moment, he had never been alone. He felt as if he might be the last angel in all the worlds.

Don't think like that. You'll lose yourself.

He tried to hold on . . . Lucinda, the roll call, Lucinda, the *choice* . . . but as he fell, it grew harder to remember. What, for instance, were the last words he'd heard spoken by the Throne—

The Gates of Heaven . . .

The Gates of Heaven are . . .

He could not remember what came next, could only dimly recall how the great light flickered, and the harshest cold swept over the Meadow, and the trees in the Orchard tumbled into one another, causing waves of furious disturbance that were felt throughout the cosmos, tsunamis of cloudsoil that blinded the angels and crushed their glory. There had been something else, something just before the obliteration of the Meadow, something like a—

Twinning.

A bold bright angel had soared up during the roll

call—said he was Daniel come back from the future. There was a sadness in his eyes that had looked so *old*. Had this angel—this . . . version of Daniel's soul—truly suffered?

Had Lucinda?

Daniel seethed with rage. He would find Lucifer, the angel who lived at the dead end of all ideas. Daniel did not fear the traitor who had been the Morning Star. Wherever, whenever they reached the end of this oblivion, Daniel would take his revenge. But first he would find Lucinda, for without her, nothing mattered. Without her love, nothing was possible.

Theirs was a love that made it inconceivable to choose Lucifer or the Throne. The only side he could ever choose was hers. So now Daniel would pay for that choice, but he did not yet understand the shape his punishment would take. Only that she was gone from the place she belonged: at his side.

The pain of separation from his soul mate coursed through Daniel suddenly, sharp and brutal. He moaned wordlessly, his mind clouded over, and suddenly, frighteningly, he couldn't remember *why*.

He tumbled onward, down through denser blackness.

He could no longer see or feel or recall how he had ended up here, nowhere, hurtling through nothingness—toward where? For how long?

His memory sputtered and faded. It was harder and harder to remember those words spoken by the angel in the white meadow who looked so much like . . .

Who had the angel resembled? And what had he said that was so important?

Daniel did not know, did not know anything anymore.

Only that he was tumbling through the void.

He was filled with an urge to find something . . . someone.

An urge to feel whole again . . .

But there was only darkness inside darkness—

Silence drowning out his thoughts—

A nothing that was everything.

Daniel fell.

ONE

THE BOOK OF THE WATCHERS

"Good morning."

A warm hand brushed Luce's cheek and tucked a strand of hair behind her ear.

Rolling onto her side, she yawned and opened her eyes. She had been sleeping deeply, dreaming about Daniel.

"Oh," she gasped, feeling her cheek. There he was.

Daniel was sitting next to her. He wore a black sweater and the same red scarf that had been knotted around his neck the first time she'd seen him at Sword & Cross. He looked better than any dream.

His weight made the edge of the cot sag a little, and Luce drew up her legs to snuggle closer to him.

"You're not a dream," she said.

Daniel's eyes were blearier than she was used to seeing them, but they still glowed the brightest violet as they gazed at her face, studying her features as if he were seeing her anew. He leaned down and pressed his lips to hers.

Luce folded into him, wrapping her arms around the back of his neck, happy to kiss him back. She didn't care that her teeth needed brushing or that she probably had bed head. She didn't care about anything other than his kiss. They were together now and neither of them could help grinning.

Then it all came rushing back:

Razor claws and dull red eyes. Choking stench of death and rot. Darkness everywhere, so complete in its doom it made light and love and everything good in the world feel tired and broken and dead.

That Lucifer had once been something else to her— Bill, the ornery stone gargoyle she'd mistaken for a friend—was impossible. She'd let him get too close, and now, because she had not done precisely as he wished— choosing not to kill her soul in ancient Egypt—he had decided to wipe the slate clean.

To bend time around to erase everything since the Fall.

Every life, every love, every moment that every mortal and angelic soul had ever experienced would be crumbled and discarded at Lucifer's reckless whim. Like the universe was a board game and he was a whining child giving up as soon as he began to lose. But what it was he wanted to win, Luce had no idea.

Her skin felt hot remembering his wrath. He'd *wanted* her to see it, to tremble in his hand when he took her back to the time of the Fall.

Then he'd thrown her aside, casting an Announcer like a net to capture all of the angels who'd fallen from Heaven.

Just as Daniel caught her in that starry noplace, Lucifer blinked out of existence, and the whole cycle started again.

It was a drastic move. Daniel explained that in order to guide the angels into the future, Lucifer would have to twin with his past self and relinquish his power. For as long as the angels took to fall, he'd be unable to do anything.

Just like the rest of them, he'd fall in powerless isolation, with his brethren but apart, together alone.

And once they fell to Earth, there would be a hiccup in time, and everything would start anew. As though the seven thousand years between then and now had never happened.

As though Luce hadn't at last begun to understand the curse.

The whole world was in jeopardy—unless Luce,

seven angels, and two Nephilim could stop him. They had just nine days and no idea where to start.

Luce had been so tired the night before that she didn't remember lying down on this cot, drawing this thin blue blanket around her shoulders. There were cobwebs in the rafters of the small cabin, a folding table cluttered with half-drunk mugs of hot chocolate that Gabbe had made for everyone last night. But it all seemed like a dream to Luce. Her flight down from the Announcer to this tiny island off Tybee, this safe zone for the angels, had been blurred by blinding exhaustion.

She'd fallen asleep while the others were still talking, letting Daniel's voice lull her into a dream. Now the cabin was quiet, and in the window behind Daniel's silhouette the sky was the gray of almost-sunrise.

She reached up to touch his cheek. He turned his head and kissed the inside of her palm. Luce squeezed her eyes to stop them from crying. Why, after all they'd been through, did Luce and Daniel have to beat the Devil before they were free to love?

"Daniel." Roland's voice called from the doorway of the cabin. His hands were tucked inside his peacoat pockets and a gray wool ski cap crowned his dreads. He gave Luce a weary smile. "It's time."

"Time for what?" Luce propped herself up on her elbows. "We're leaving? Already? What about my parents? They're probably panicked."

"I thought I'd take you by their house now," Daniel said, "to say goodbye."

"But how am I going to explain disappearing after Thanksgiving dinner?"

She remembered Daniel's words last night: Though it felt like they'd been inside the Announcers for an eternity, in real time only a few hours had passed.

Still, to Harry and Doreen Price, a few hours of a missing daughter *was* eternity.

Daniel and Roland shared a glance. "We took care of it," Roland said, handing Daniel a set of car keys.

"You took care of it how?" Luce asked. "My dad once called the police when I was half an hour late from school—"

"Don't worry, kid," Roland said. "We've got you covered. You just need to make a quick costume change." He pointed toward a backpack on the rocking chair by the door. "Gabbe brought over your things."

"Um, thanks," she said, confused. Where was Gabbe? Where were the rest of them? The cabin had been packed the night before, positively cozy with the glow of angel wings and the smell of hot chocolate and cinnamon. The memory of that coziness, coupled with the promise of saying goodbye to her parents without knowing where she was going, made this morning feel empty.

The wood floor was rough against her bare feet. Looking down, she realized she was still wearing the narrow white shift dress she'd had on in Egypt, the last life she'd visited through the Announcers. Bill had made her wear it.

No, not Bill. *Lucifer*. He'd leered so approvingly as she tucked the starshot into her waistband, contemplating the advice he'd given her on how to kill her soul.

Never, never, never. Luce had too much to live for.

Inside the old green backpack she used to take to summer camp, Luce found her favorite pair of pajamas—the red-and-white-striped flannel set—neatly folded, with the matching white slippers underneath. "But it's morning," she said. "What do I need pajamas for?"

Again Daniel and Roland shared a glance, and this time, Luce could swear they were trying not to laugh.

"Just trust us," Roland said.

After she was dressed, Luce followed Daniel out of the cabin, letting his broad shoulders buffer the wind as they walked down the pebbly shore to the water.

The tiny island off Tybee was about a mile from the Savannah coastline. Across that stretch of sea, Roland had promised that a car was waiting.

Daniel's wings were concealed, but he must have sensed her eyeing the place where they unfurled from his shoulders. "When everything is in order, we'll fly wherever we have to go to stop Lucifer. Until then it's better to stay low to the ground."

"Okay," Luce said.

"Race you to the other side?"

Her breath frosted the air. "You know I'd beat you."

"True." He slipped an arm around her waist, warming her. "Maybe we'd better take the boat, then. Protect my famous pride."

She watched him unmoor a small metal rowboat from a single boat slip. The soft light on the water made her think back to the day they'd raced across the secret lake at Sword & Cross. His skin had glistened as they had pulled themselves up to the flat rock in the center to catch their breaths, then had lain on the sun-warmed stone, letting the day's heat dry their bodies. She'd barely known Daniel then—she hadn't known he was an angel—and already she'd been dangerously in love with him.

"We used to swim together in my lifetime in Tahiti, didn't we?" she asked, surprised to remember another time she'd seen Daniel's hair glistening with water.

Daniel stared at her and she knew how much it meant to him to finally be able to share some of his memories of their past. He looked so moved that Luce thought he might cry.

Instead he kissed her forehead tenderly and said, "You beat me all those times, too, Lulu."

They didn't talk much as Daniel rowed. It was enough for Luce just to watch the way his muscles strained and flexed each time he dragged the oars back, hearing them dip in and out of the cold water, breathing in the brine of the ocean. The sun was rising over her shoulders, warming the back of her neck, but as they approached the mainland, she saw something that sent a shiver down her spine.

A car. She recognized the white Taurus immediately.

"What's wrong?" Daniel saw Luce's posture stiffen as the rowboat touched the shore. "Oh. That." He sounded unconcerned as he hopped out of the boat and held out a hand to Luce. The ground was mulchy and rich-smelling. It reminded Luce of her childhood.

"It's not what you think," Daniel said. "When Sophia fled Sword and Cross, after"—Luce waited, wincing, hoping Daniel wouldn't say *after she murdered Penn*—"after we found out who she really was, the angels confiscated her car." His face hardened. "She owes us that much, and more."

Luce thought of Penn's white face, the blood draining from it. "Where is Sophia now?"

Daniel shook his head. "I don't know. Unfortunately, we'll probably soon find out. I have a feeling she'll worm her way into our plans." He drew the keys from his pocket, inserted one into the passenger door. "But that's not what you should be worried about right now."

"Okay." Luce squinted at him as she sank onto the gray cloth seat. "So there's something *else* I should be worried about right now?"

Daniel turned the key, and the car shuddered slowly

to life. The last time she'd sat in this seat, she'd been worried about being in the car alone with him. It was the first night they'd ever kissed—as far as she'd known then, anyway. She was stabbing at the seat belt when she felt his fingers over hers. "Remember," he said softly, reaching over to buckle her belt, letting his hands linger over hers. "There's a trick."

He kissed her softly on the cheek, then put the car in drive and peeled out of the wet woods onto the narrow two-lane blacktop. They were the only ones on the road.

"Daniel?" Luce asked again. "What else should I be worried about?"

He glanced at her pajamas. "How good are you at playing sick?"

⁂

The white Taurus idled in the alley behind her parents' house as Luce crept past the three azalea trees beside her bedroom window. In the summer, there would be tomato vines creeping out of the black soil, but in winter the side yard looked barren and dreary and not very much like home. She couldn't remember the last time she'd stood out here. She'd sneaked out of three different boarding schools before, but never out of her own parents' house. Now she was sneaking *in,* and she didn't even know how her window worked. Luce looked around at what she could see of her sleepy neighborhood, at the morning paper sitting in its dewy plastic bag at the edge of her parents' lawn, at the old, netless basketball hoop in the Johnsons' driveway across the street. Nothing had changed since she'd been gone. Nothing had changed, except Luce. If Bill succeeded, would this neighborhood vanish, too?

She gave one last wave to Daniel, who was watching from the car, took a deep breath, and used her thumbs to pry the lower panel from the cracking blue paint of the sill.

It slid right up. Someone inside had already popped out the screen. Luce paused, stunned as the white muslin curtains parted and the half-blond, half-black head of her onetime enemy Molly Zane filled the open space.

"'Sup, Meat Loaf."

Luce bristled at the nickname she'd earned on her first day at Sword & Cross. *This* was what Daniel and Roland meant when they said they'd taken care of things at home?

"What are you doing here, Molly?"

"Come on. I won't bite." Molly extended a hand. Her nails were chipped, emerald green.

Luce sank her hand into Molly's, ducked and sidled, one leg at a time, through the window.

Her bedroom looked small and outdated, like a time capsule left by some long-ago Luce. There was the framed poster of the Eiffel Tower on the back of her door. There was her bulletin board full of swim team ribbons from Thunderbolt Elementary. And there, under the green-and-yellow Hawaiian-print duvet, was her best friend, Callie.

Callie scrambled from under the covers, dashed around the bed, and flung herself into Luce's arms. "They kept telling me you were going to be okay, but in that lying, we're-all-so-completely-terrified-we're-just-not-going-to-explain-a-word-to-you kind of way. Do you even realize how thoroughly creepy that was? It was like you physically dropped off the face of the earth—"

Luce hugged her back tightly. As far as Callie knew, Luce had only been gone since the night before.

"Okay, you two," Molly growled, pulling Luce away from Callie, "you can OMG your faces off later. I didn't lie in your bed in that cheap polyester wig all night pretending to be Luce with stomach flu so you guys could blow our cover now." She rolled her eyes. "Amateurs."

"Hold on. You did what?" Luce asked.

"After you . . . disappeared," Callie said breathlessly, "we knew we could never explain it to your parents. I mean, I could barely fathom it after seeing it with my own eyes. So I told them you felt sick and had gone to bed and Molly pretended to be you and—"

"Lucky I found this in your closet." Molly twirled a short, wavy black wig around one finger. "Halloween remnant?"

"Wonder Woman." Luce winced, regretting her middle school Halloween costume, and not for the first time.

"Well, it worked."

It was strange to see Molly—who'd once sided with Lucifer—helping her. But even Molly, like Cam and Roland, didn't want to fall again. So here they were, a team.

"You covered for me? I don't know what to say. Thank you."

"Whatever." Molly jerked her head at Callie; anything to deflect Luce's gratitude. "She was the real silver-tongued devil. Thank her." She stuck one leg out of the open window and turned to call back, "Think you guys can handle it from here? I have a summit meeting at Waffle House."

Luce gave Molly a thumbs-up and flopped down on her bed.

"Oh, Luce," Callie whispered. "When you left, your whole backyard was covered in this gray *dust*. And that blond girl, Gabbe, swept her hand once and made it *disappear*. Then we said you were sick, that everyone else had gone home, and we just started doing the dishes with your parents. And at first I thought that Molly girl was a little bit terrible, but she's actually kind of cool." Her eyes narrowed. "But where *did* you go? What happened to you? You *scared* me."

"I don't even know where to start," Luce said. "I'm sorry."

There was a knock, followed by the familiar creak of her bedroom door opening.

Luce's mother stood in the hallway, her sleep-wild hair pulled back by a yellow banana clip, her face bare of makeup and pretty. She was holding a wicker tray with two glasses of orange juice, two plates of buttered toast, and a box of Alka-Seltzer. "Looks like someone's feeling better."

Luce waited for her mom to put the tray down on the nightstand; then she wrapped her arms around her mother's waist and buried her face in her pink terry-cloth bathrobe. Tears stung her eyes. She sniffed.

"My little girl," her mom said, feeling Luce's fore-head and cheeks to check for fever. She hadn't used that soft, sweet voice with Luce in ages, and it felt so good to hear.

"I love you, Mom."

"Don't tell me she's too sick for Black Friday." Luce's father appeared in the doorway, holding a green plastic watering can. He was smiling, but behind his rimless glasses, his eyes looked concerned.

"I am feeling better," Luce said, "but—"

"Oh, Harry," Luce's mom said. "You know we only had her for the day. She has to be back at school." She turned to Luce. "Daniel called a little while ago, honey. He said he can pick you up and take you back to school. I said that of course your father and I would be happy to, but—"

"No," Luce said quickly, remembering the plan Daniel had detailed in the car. "You guys should go do your Black Friday shopping. It's a Price family tradition."

They agreed that Luce would ride with Daniel, and her parents would take Callie to the airport. While the girls ate their breakfast, Luce's parents sat on the edge of the bed and talked about Thanksgiving ("Gabbe polished all the china—what an angel"). By the time they moved on to the Black Friday deals they were on the hunt for ("All your father ever wants is tools"), Luce realized that she hadn't said anything except for inane conversational fillers like "Uh-huh" and "Oh, really?"

When her parents finally stood up to take the plates into the kitchen, and Callie started to pack, Luce went into the bathroom and shut the door.

She was alone for the first time in what seemed like a million ages. She sat down on the vanity stool and looked in the mirror.

She was herself, but different. Sure, Lucinda Price looked back at her. But also . . .

There was Layla in the fullness of her lips, Lulu in the thick waves of her hair, Lu Xin's intensity in the hazel of her eyes, Lucia's dimple in her cheek, ready for mischief. She was not alone. Maybe she never would be alone again. There, in the mirror, was every incarnation of Lucinda staring back at her and wondering, *What is to become of us? What about our history, and our love?*

She took a shower and put on clean jeans, her black riding boots, and a long white sweater. She sat down on Callie's suitcase while her friend struggled to zip it up. The silence between them was brutal.

"You're my best friend, Callie," Luce finally said. "I'm going through something I don't understand. But that thing isn't you. I'm sorry I don't know how to be more specific, but I've missed you. So much."

Callie's shoulders tensed. "You used to tell me everything." But the look that passed between them suggested both girls knew that wasn't possible anymore.

A car door slammed out front.

Through the open blinds Luce watched Daniel make his way up her parents' path. And even though it had been less than an hour since he had dropped her off, Luce felt her cheeks flush at the sight of him. He walked slowly, as if he were floating, his red scarf trailing behind him in the wind. Even Callie stared.

Luce's parents stood together in the foyer. She hugged each one of them for a long time—Dad first, then Mom, then Callie, who squeezed her hard and whispered quickly, "What I saw you do last night was beautiful. I just want you to know that."

Luce felt her eyes burn again. She squeezed Callie back and mouthed *thank you*.

Then she walked down the path and into Daniel's arms and whatever came along with them.

"There you are, you lovebirds you, doin' that thing that lovebirds do," Arriane sang, bobbing her head out from behind a long bookcase. She was sitting cross-legged on a wooden library chair, juggling a few Hacky Sacks. She wore overalls and combat boots, and her dark hair was plaited into tiny pigtails.

Luce was not overjoyed to be back at the Sword & Cross library. It had been renovated since the fire that destroyed it, but it still smelled like something big and ugly had burned there. The faculty had explained away the fire as a freak accident, but someone had been killed—Todd, a quiet student Luce had barely known until the night he died—and Luce knew there was something darker lurking beneath the surface of the story. She blamed herself.

Now, as she and Daniel rounded the corner of a bookshelf and headed for the library's study area, Luce saw that Arriane was not alone. All of them were there: Gabbe, Roland, Cam, Molly, Annabelle—the leggy angel with the hot-pink hair—even Miles and Shelby, who waved excitedly and looked decidedly different from the other angels, but also different from mortal teens.

Miles and Shelby were—were they holding *hands*? But when she looked again, their hands had disappeared under the table they were all sitting at. Miles tugged his baseball cap lower. Shelby cleared her throat and hunched lower over a book.

"Your book," Luce said to Daniel as soon as she spotted the thick spine with the brown crumbling glue near the bottom. The faded cover read *The Watchers: Myth in Medieval Europe by Daniel Grigori*.

Her hand reached automatically for the pale gray cover. She closed her eyes because it reminded her of Penn, who shouldn't have died; and because the photograph pasted inside the front cover of the book was the first thing that had convinced her that what Daniel told her about their history might be possible.

It was a photograph taken from another life, one in Helston, England. And even though it shouldn't have been possible, there was no doubt about it: The young woman in the photograph was Lucinda Price.

"Where did you find it?" Luce asked.

Her voice must have given something away, because Shelby said, "What is so major about this dusty old thing anyway?"

"It's precious. Our only key now," Gabbe said. "Sophia tried to burn it once."

"Sophia?" Luce's hand shot to her heart. "Miss Sophia tried—the fire in the library? That was her?" The others nodded. "She killed Todd," Luce said numbly.

So it *hadn't* been Luce's fault. Another life to lay at Sophia's feet.

"And she almost died of shock the night you showed it to her," Roland said. "We were all shocked, especially when you lived to talk about it."

"We talked about Daniel kissing me," Luce remembered, blushing. "And the fact that I survived it. Was that what surprised Miss Sophia?"

"Part of it," Roland said. "But there's plenty more in that book that Sophia wouldn't have wanted you to know about."

"Not much of an educator, was she?" Cam said.

"What wouldn't she have wanted me to know?"

All the angels turned to look at Daniel.

"Last night we told you that none of the angels remember where we landed when we fell," Daniel said.

"Yeah, about that. How's it possible?" Shelby said. "You'd think that kind of thing would leave an impression on the old memorizer."

Cam's face reddened. "You try falling for nine days through multiple dimensions and trillions of miles, landing on your face, breaking your wings, rolling around concussed for who knows how long, wandering the desert for decades looking for any clue as to who or what or where you are—and then talk to me about the old memorizer."

"Okay, you've got issues," Shelby said, putting on her shrink voice. "If *I* were going to diagnose you—"

"Well, at least you remember there was a desert involved," Miles said diplomatically, making Shelby laugh.

Daniel turned to Luce. "I wrote this book after I lost you in Tibet . . . but before I'd met you in Prussia. I know you visited that life in Tibet because I followed you there, so maybe you can see how losing you like I did made me turn to years of research and study to find a way out of this curse."

Luce looked down. That death had made Daniel run straight off a cliff. She feared its happening again.

"Cam is right," Daniel said. "None of us recall where we landed. We wandered the desert until it was no longer desert, we wandered the plains and the valleys and the seas until they *turned* to desert. It wasn't until we slowly found one another and began to piece together the story that we remembered we'd ever been angels at all.

"But there were relics of our Fall, records that mankind found and kept as treasures, gifts—they think—from a god they don't understand. For a long time the relics were buried in a temple in Jerusalem, but during the Crusades, they were stolen, spirited away to various places. None of us knew where.

"When I did my research, I focused on the medieval era, turning to as many resources as I could in a kind of theological scavenger hunt for the relics. The gist of it is that if these three artifacts can be collected and gathered together at Mount Sinai—"

"Why Mount Sinai?" Shelby asked.

"The channels between the Throne and the Earth are

closest there," Gabbe explained with a flip of her hair. "That's where Moses received the Ten Commandments, that's where the angels enter when they're delivering messages from the Throne."

"Think of it as God's local dive," Arriane added, sending a Hacky Sack too high in the air and into an overhead lamp.

"But before you ask," Cam said, making a point to single out Shelby with his eyes, "Mount Sinai is not the original site of the Fall."

"That would be way too easy," Annabelle said.

"If the relics are all gathered at Mount Sinai," Daniel said, "then, in theory, the location of the Fall will be revealed."

"In theory." Cam sneered. "Must I be the one to say there is some question regarding the validity of Daniel's research—"

Daniel clenched his jaw. "You have a better idea?"

"Don't you think"—Cam raised his voice—"that your theory puts rather a lot of weight on the idea that these relics are anything more than rumor? Who knows if they can do what they're supposed to do?"

Luce studied the group of angels and demons—her only allies in this quest to save herself and Daniel . . . and the world. "So that unknown location is where we have to be nine days from now."

"*Less* than nine days from now," Daniel said. "Nine

days from now will be too late. Lucifer—and the host of angels cast out of Heaven—will have arrived."

"But if we can beat Lucifer to the site of the Fall," Luce said, "then what?"

Daniel shook his head. "We don't really know. I never told anyone about this book because I didn't know what it would add up to, and without you being there to play your part—"

"*My* part?" Luce asked.

"Which we don't really yet understand—"

Gabbe elbowed Daniel, cutting him off. "What he means is, all will be revealed in time."

Molly smacked her forehead. "Really? 'All will be revealed'? Is that all you guys know? Is *that* what you're going on?"

"That and *your* importance," Cam said to Luce. "You're the chess piece they're fighting over here."

"What?" Luce whispered.

"Shut up," Daniel said to Cam, then fixed his attention on Luce. "Don't listen to him."

Cam snorted, but no one acknowledged it. His disdain just sat in the room like an uninvited guest. The angels and demons were silent. No one was going to leak anything else about Luce's role in stopping the Fall.

"So all of this information, this scavenger hunt," she said, "it's in that book?"

"More or less," Daniel said. "I just have to spend some time with the text to know where we begin."

The others moved away to give Daniel space at the table. Luce felt Miles's hand brush the back of her arm. They'd barely spoken since she'd come back through the Announcer.

"Can I talk to you?" Miles asked, very quietly. "Luce?"

The strained look on his face made Luce think of those last few moments in her parents' backyard, when Miles had thrown her reflection.

They'd never really talked about the kiss they'd shared on the roof outside her Shoreline dorm room. Surely Miles knew it was a mistake—but why did Luce feel like she was leading him on every time she was nice to him?

"Luce." It was Gabbe, appearing at Miles's side. "I thought I'd mention"—she glanced at Miles—"if you wanted to go visit Penn for a moment, now would be the time."

"Good idea." Luce nodded. "Thanks." She glanced apologetically at Miles, but he just tugged his baseball cap over his eyes and turned to whisper something to Shelby.

"Ahem." Shelby coughed indignantly. She was standing behind Daniel, trying to read the book over his shoulder. "What about me and Miles?"

"You're going back to Shoreline," Gabbe said, sounding more like Luce's teachers at Shoreline than Luce had ever noticed before. "We need you to alert Steven and Francesca. We may need their help—and your help, too. Tell them"—she took a deep breath—"tell them it's happening. That an endgame has come to pass, though not as we'd expected. Tell them everything. They will know what to do."

"Fine," Shelby said, scowling. "You're the boss."

"*Yodelayhee-hooooo.*" Arriane cupped her palms around her mouth. "If, uh, Luce wants to get out, someone's gonna have to help her down from the window." She thrummed her fingers on the table, looking sheepish. "I made a library-book barricade near the entrance in case any of the Sword and Cross-eyeds felt inclined to disrupt us."

"Dibs." Cam already had his arm slipped through the crook of Luce's elbow. She started to argue, but none of the other angels seemed to think it was a bad idea. Daniel didn't even notice.

Near the back exit, Shelby and Miles both mouthed *Be careful* to Luce, with varying degrees of fierceness.

Cam walked her to the window, radiating warmth with his smile. He slid the glass pane up and together they looked out at the campus where they'd met, where they'd grown close, where he'd tricked her into kissing him. They weren't all bad memories. . . .

He hopped through the window first, landing smoothly on the ledge, and held out a hand for hers.

"Milady."

His grip was strong, and it made her feel tiny and weightless as he drifted down from the ledge, two stories in two seconds. His wings were concealed, but he still moved as gracefully as if he were flying. They landed softly on the dewy grass.

"I take it you don't want my company," he said. "At the cemetery—not, you know, in general."

"Right. No, thanks."

He looked away and reached into his pocket, pulled out a tiny silver bell. It looked ancient and had Hebrew writing on it. He handed it to her. "Just ring when you want a hand back up."

"Cam," Luce said. "What is my role in all of this?"

Cam reached out to touch her cheek, then seemed to think better of it. His hand hovered in the air. "Daniel's right. It isn't our place to tell you."

He didn't wait for her response—just bent his knees and soared off the ground. He didn't even look back.

Luce stared at the campus for a moment, letting the familiar Sword & Cross humidity stick to her skin. She couldn't tell whether the dismal school, with its huge, harsh neo-Gothic buildings and sad, defeated landscaping, looked different or the same.

She strolled across the campus, across the flat, still grass of the commons, past the depressing dormitory, to the wrought iron gate of the cemetery. There she paused, feeling goose bumps rise on her arms.

The cemetery still looked and smelled like a sinkhole in the middle of the campus. The dust from the angels' battle had cleared. It was still early enough that most of the students were asleep, and anyway, none of them were likely to be prowling the cemetery, unless they were serving detention. She let herself in through the gate and ambled down through the leaning headstones and the muddy graves.

In the far east corner lay Penn's final resting place. Luce sat down at the foot of her friend's plot. She didn't have flowers and she didn't know any prayers, so she laid her hands on the cold, wet grass, closed her eyes, and sent her own kind of message to Penn, worrying that it might never reach her.

❊

Luce got back to the library window feeling irritable. She didn't need Cam or his bell to rescue her. She could get up to the ledge by herself.

It was easy enough to scale the lowest portion of the sloped roof, and from there she could climb up a few levels until she was close to the long, narrow ledge beneath the library windows. It was about two feet wide. As she crept along it, Cam's and Daniel's bickering voices wafted outside.

"What if one of us were to be intercepted?" Cam's

voice was high and pleading. "You know we are stronger united, Daniel."

"If we don't make it there in time, our strength won't matter. We'll be *erased*."

She could picture them on the other side of the wall: Cam with fists clenched and green eyes flashing, Daniel stolid and immovable, with his arms crossed over his chest.

"I don't trust you not to act on your own behalf." Cam's tone was harsh.

"There's nothing to discuss." Daniel didn't change his tone. "Splitting up is our only option."

The others were quiet, probably thinking the same thing Luce was. She reached the window and saw that the two angels were facing each other. Cam and Daniel behaved far too much like brothers for anyone else to dare come between them.

Luce's hands gripped the windowsill. She felt a small swell of pride—which she would never confess—at having made it back into the library without help. Probably none of the angels would even notice. She sighed and slid one leg inside. That was when the window began to shudder.

The glass rattled in its pane, and the sill gyrated in her hands with such force she was almost knocked off the ledge. She held on tighter, feeling vibrations inside her, as if her heart and her soul were trembling, too.

"Earthquake," she whispered. Her foot skimmed the back of the ledge just as her grip on the windowsill loosened.

"Lucinda!"

Daniel rushed to the window. His hands found their way around hers. Cam was there, too, one hand on the base of Luce's shoulders, another on the back of her head. The bookshelves rippled and the lights in the library flickered as the two angels pulled her through the rocking window just before the pane slipped from the frame and shattered into a thousand shards of glass.

She looked to Daniel for a clue. He was still gripping her wrists, but his eyes traveled past her, outside. He was watching the sky, which had turned angry and gray.

Worse than all of that was the lingering vibration *inside* Luce, which made her feel as if she'd been electrocuted. It seemed like an eternity, but it lasted for five, maybe ten seconds—enough time for Luce, Cam, and Daniel to fall to the dusty wooden floor of the library with a thud.

Then the trembling stopped and the world grew deathly quiet.

"What the hell?" Arriane picked herself up off the floor. "Did we step through to California without my knowledge? No one told me there were fault lines in Georgia!"

Cam pulled a long shard of glass from his forearm.

Luce gasped as bright red blood trailed down his elbow, but his face showed no sign that he was in pain. "That wasn't an earthquake. That was a seismic shift in time."

"A *what*?" Luce asked.

"The first of many." Daniel looked out the jagged window, watching a white cumulus cloud roll across the now-blue sky. "The closer Lucifer gets, the stronger they'll become." He glanced at Cam, who nodded.

"Tick-tock, people," Cam said. "Time's running out. We need to fly."

VISIT FALLENBOOKS.CO.UK FOR THE LATEST FALLEN NEWS.

EXCERPT COPYRIGHT © 2012 BY TINDERBOX BOOKS, LLC AND LAUREN KATE.

PUBLISHED IN GREAT BRITAIN BY DOUBLEDAY

AN IMPRINT OF RANDOM HOUSE CHILDREN'S BOOKS

A RANDOM HOUSE GROUP COMPANY

LAUREN KATE is the internationally bestselling author of *The Betrayal of Natalie Hargrove* and the Fallen novels: *Fallen, Torment, Passion,* and the forthcoming *Rapture.* Her books have been translated into more than thirty languages. She lives in Los Angeles with her husband. You can visit her online at: laurenkatebooks.net.